With the Sound of the Sea

Also by Charlotte Fairbairn

God Breathes His Dreams Through Nathaniel Cadwallader

With the Sound of the Sea

Charlotte Fairbairn

review

First published in 2003
by REVIEW

An imprint of Headline Book Publishing

First published in paperback in 2004

10 9 8 7 6 5 4 3 2 1

Cataloguing in Publication Data is available
from the British Library

ISBN 0 7553 0185 4

Typeset in Minion by Palimpsest Book Production Limited,
Polmont, Stirlingshire
Printed and bound in Great Britain by
Clays Ltd, St Ives plc

Headline Book Publishing
A division of Hodder Headline
338 Euston Road
London NW1 3BH

www.reviewbooks.co.uk
www.hodderheadline.com

This novel was inspired in part by a visit to New Zealand. It is dedicated to Sonja, who lived and died there; and to Piha, the beach she visited with her brothers every summer as a child.

Acknowledgements

Without Simon Trewin, Mary-Anne Harrington, my mother Elizabeth Fairbairn and my husband Ross Pople, the sound of the sea would not have been heard. Their support is deeply felt.

Part One

One

A stickleback whirls through a soft white wind. It soars, swings, supple as a butterfly. Athene Brown is sitting on her father's lap and she watches, head tipped back, as the fish loops slowly down towards her. It lands on her knee. The stickleback's complex architecture of fins imprints itself on Athene Brown as she runs her fingers along its tiny form. For a fragment of time she is entranced.

The stickleback is followed by another, then another; by a handful of minnows and a handful of small white crabs; by a clutch of sprats and then some more and soon the air above Athene Brown's seven-year-old head is glinting, filled with fins and tails, with white and blue and ocean-silver flashes. Athene Brown's eyes widen. It is raining fish.

The soft white wind changes to something darker, stronger. The fish multiply and the air fills with water and bits of seaweed. Now the fish are bigger and mackerel, herring, snapper, grouper start to plop to earth and their lips are smacking because the ground around is dry, not water as it should be.

Athene Brown raises her arms above her head to protect

herself from the thuds of all the fish that are tumbling out of the sky. She shifts, pressing herself deeper into him. The blow of the wind pulls on her hair, squashes down on her chest like so many heavy stones, and she shifts again, leans close against him, clings to his chest until she can hear his heartbeat thudding like hers. She tries to wipe her eyes because the wind is sucking sharp tears out of her ducts. She tries to catch her breath, to shout out, she tries to see through the dark air around her, she wants to put out her hand and stop it, stop, but there is so much noise, she can hear nothing, do nothing.

And then she does see – she looks down to the ground and she sees how the sand is a carpet of fish and they are all gasping and they are all dying. Their eyes are looking at her and their fins are flapping at her and Athene Brown feels a hot child-rush of indignation which eclipses her fear. She slithers down from his lap. She tries to scoop them up and they are like wet pebbles or bars of soap, so difficult to catch, so tricky to hold onto. She puts a few in a bucket. Then a few more. Her hands are icy, her arms are frozen. A frog flies into her hair, catching her in the eye as it does so. An eel hits her on the chest. She fights to stay upright because this wind, it is fierce, it is determined to suck her up as it has already done with all those fish.

And so Athene Brown is forced to sit down once more – on the ground by his feet – and she shouts out Papa-help-me and she bites into his leg, trying to make him pay attention, trying to make him help her save all those fish.

The storm soon passes. Some of the fish survive – Athene

Brown remembers bucketing them herself, frantic, small, panic-stricken. She remembers sliding them with her bare feet and pushing them with her hands and scooping them up and she does not want to know that her father has not helped her, he should have, the fish are all dead and dying, it is very bad.

At last some others from the huts come out to help. They join in, fingers, hands, feet, buckets, awestruck by the storm but at the same time dealing urgently, erratically, with its consequences. There is chatter and the sky slowly clears. There are voices and squealing and the rattle of handles. The slap-slap of the fish waxes, then eventually wanes as the winds blow off into the sea, as the rains ebb and the tides regain their rhythm.

Years later Athene Brown can still draw with her eyes shut the pattern of a stickleback's fins. She can trace its lines and the ups and downs of its profile. She remembers the swish that it makes as it, the first, tumbles through the wind and onto her knee. She remembers the tall dark of the sky above and the incredible whirring menace as the storm gathers pace. She remembers the cricks of the crabs as some of them hit rocks and the plops of the larger fish as they land one on top of the other like raindrops. She remembers the twist in the air, how things just disappear upwards into it, how the water comes up and goes down and it was all just so much magic, all so long ago.

And too, she can recall his smell – the smell of his hair and his skin and the feel of his hand as it cups her leg, holding her firm, holding her kind and strong. She can bring back the timbre of his voice which always, every time she thinks of it, takes her to a place that is both challenging and reassuring – a voice that is gritty, a voice that carries the song of the sea and the roar of the hot sea-winds.

And still, every time she travels this journey, every time she traces the silhouette of Isaiah the fisherman, Isaiah her father, she finds herself fighting to wipe her eyes – her tears falling faster than the fish, sharper than the wind, longer than the streams of eels. For her memory traces its long slow progress to his face and all she can remember is the blank – blank-blank – and he looks like one of the fish that did not survive, one of the fish that was starved of breath by the storm.

They call it Samuel's Bay because it was Samuel who first lived here, eighty, maybe a hundred years ago. Samuel the warrior. Samuel the hermit. Samuel who discovered the beach when there was still no road and the bay was so hidden, so hard to reach that you might never know of its existence.

By the time Isaiah's forebears arrived, the old man had become the stuff of legends. Children sang of his triumphant feats and his crusading spirit; they sang of him as they might of a giant or a fairy-tale ogre – his deeds were magnified beyond all possible truth and his character was painted dark and dangerous, demonic and hell-bent.

But in his own day, all Samuel was was a man – a man who needed to do what he needed to do. He needed a secret place because he was better alone. He needed a kingdom because, in his small way, he was a king, a man with vision, a fighter. Away from the madding crowds, off the track beaten by lesser mortals. And he saw, behind those trees, through that scrub, at the end of that tortuous, overgrown, foot-wide ridge, that here was a place and he knew at once that here he could live and be in peace.

How old was Samuel when he discovered the bay? How old was he when he fought the war of the path? The legends do not tell. They speak of a man with a black cloak and a long burr-pipe. They speak of a man who eschewed the company of men, who barely spoke, who was stooped and wizened and strange. They speak many things of Samuel, some no doubt closer to the truth than others.

But they do not sing the song of his first arrival in that bay, they cannot because they could never imagine how it was to fight through those bushes, to beat them back for days, weeks, months; how it was when the thorn grabbed at his clothes, when the ground snapped at his feet, when his back threatened to break under the strain of being bent double for so many days, weeks, months; how it was when the sunlight disappeared for yards on end, when the wind stung and the rain fell, when all sense of direction disappeared in the face of this unnegotiable thicket; how he made the path, willed the path, ducked the thorn, carved out those miles of craggy foothold, held his breath, mopped his brow, pressed on and on – and then emerged into a place which he knew, with his chin and his will and his strength, he knew must have been there all along.

And the songs could never possibly capture that moment when, bloodied, exhausted, worn to a pile of bones, Samuel walked out upon the iron-black sand and he was in a place of such blessed contrast: so dark the sand, so blue the sea, so fierce the sun, so tall the Lion Rock that jutted up in the middle of the beach and made long shadows in its wake. Smelt the trees, the wisping reedy grass, saw the dunes, felt the wind as it whipped his hair, thought this is where I will stay, this is where I will be free; dropped his arms, his lungs, his heart on the sand and spun in a circle, spun until there was a dipping hole around him – a hole that would never release him until his dying day.

Stand on the top of the Lion Rock – like Samuel, like Ezekiel, like Isaiah, like Athene Brown – and describe the circle of the bay. Look with your wind-battered eyes at the ridge of hills that surrounds it. These hills, they hug the bay – a soft rippling embrace. They shroud the bay, keep her apart, private, shielded. On the one side, their slopes are gentle and they lead long and slowly into the yawning buff velvet of the plain; and on this, they are sheer yet craggy, pitted with crevasses that have been gouged out during the sudden floods of the rainy season, then softened by the constant barrage of the wind.

Stringing along the top of the ridge a line of trees – conifers, pointed or domed – marking out pertly this place from that, this ridge from that. And then beneath there is forest, true scrub growth, and here the primness of the conifers is undermined by the vast range of shrubs, palms, bushes, weeds which have seeded themselves in some incomprehensible, motley pattern. Trees with cones, trees with feathers, trees with huge pods that swing indolently from the branches. Trees with trunks fat at the bottom, trees with roots which seem to sprout from the top – and beneath all this, a carpet of purple grass which is tall and wispy and razor-sharp so that if you walk through it with bare legs, you emerge, calves bleeding.

The place is sinew, the ground wafting and waving, back and forth, with the steady pounding of the wind. The place is texture, you want to reach out and feel it, the sharp parts, the soft parts, blowy, winnowy like the hairs of a bear's coat. In spring a form of gorse with lemon-fragrant flowers blooms and makes the beach glow with a gorgeous citrus smell. And all year long, dark against light, tall against low. The wind, the sea, the hills, the cutty-grass – in the centre of it all, the Lion himself, rearing up with spittle dripping from his colossal jaws.

Of course it had been there for a thousand years. Of course all the fishermen who came round that point had known about this Eden as they had known about all the pockets of paradise scattered up and down this western coastline of their island. From the waters, they could see the sand and the embrace of the hills, they could see the soaring monolith of the Lion, they could see the soft wig of the cutty-grass and the round bosoms of the dunes. But they could never venture there, not into this bay – because too many men before them had been smashed to their death on the Deadmen.

How many rocks were there in this terrible chain? Few fishermen could agree. When the tide was low, they poked menacingly through the surface of the waves like sea-monsters. When the tide was high, there was no chance of being able to tell how many or how big and all there was to see were eddying swirls of current and a disconcerting stillness in the waters beyond. As a young boy, Isaiah used to try to swim out to the Deadmen, to map them in his mind so he would know one day how to navigate around them – but the Deadmen were not just fierce, they were cunning also. By dint of channels beneath and channels through the rock, they had a capacity to suck down as well as inwards and Isaiah soon found out what many fishermen's families already knew to their cost – that these rocks had earned their name, that they deserved their fearsome reputation.

When Samuel first arrived, the Deadmen had spat the bones of their latest victim out onto the beach. Blood-red fragments from the hull of a fishing-boat lay scattered along the sand. There was no sign of its occupant but Samuel did not mind too much, he saw the possibilities, put down his cloak on the iron-black sand, got to work, gathered in the wood piece by piece. He took a stone, took out his knife, carved some pegs, found some string, a spade, some rocks, built himself a hut so he could shelter from the sea and from the beating winds.

Slowly, thanks to the greed of the Deadmen, Samuel came to elaborate on his red hut. He roofed it with tin, added a chimney stack, windows of sorts, a door. When the hours dragged on, he carved coloured driftwood in long repeating patterns – shells or fish or boats or women linking hands. He fastened them along the overhang of the roof, round the door, the frames of the windows. He laced it with patterns, lavishing all the care that he did not bestow upon the waters on the constant elaboration of his scarlet shanty.

Those who survived the eddying waters of the rocks used to look back at Samuel's hut and admire, even from a distance, its intricate woodwork. The red stood out like a fire, the tin when he had polished it blinded them in the sun. His was a kind of lighthouse and they knew that if they could make out the detail too well, they were probably edging perilously close to those savage, man-battering rocks.

You might ask why they kept trying. You might ask why they did not learn the lesson of the Deadmen, why year in, year out there were boats and hulls, oars and fishermen battered upon those rocks. You might think that the red of Samuel's hut would act as sufficient warning, like a dead rat hanging on a fence, that they would stop veering too close to Samuel's Bay. But the truth is that the temptation to enter the bay was always there, always lurking just the other side of those rocks. It could have been nuggets of gold or lumps of coral or rocks of unhewn diamond so large that they would not fit into the palm of his hand.

But it was none of these. It was fish.

If you stood on the Lion Rock with its view all round, enfolded in the arms of the bay, you could watch them string through the sea like necklaces. If you walked through the waters with your bare, dark legs, you could feel them tickling you, fins on fins on fins. If you rolled your head back on your shoulders, let your hair lift in the endless winds, still you could hear them as they snaked through the waters – shoals upon shoals of fish. There were so many that the sky would be alive, a gentle lightning, silver flashing with cloudless whispering light. There were so many that the waters in those days shimmered, always restless, and even fishermen who had watched their sons dying among the Deadmen, even they kept trying to sail through, to sail under the shadow of the Lion Rock into the lilac curve of the waters, into the seething millions of all those fish.

Samuel stepped out of his hut on the beach, he climbed the Lion Rock, he sat and looked out over the necklaces of fish. Sometimes, he walked among them. He let them brush against his shins while he stalked through the shallows, burr-pipe in hand. Sometimes he rowed out beyond the bay – for the pleasure of being able to return, to see them all there, sun glinting on the water, reflecting off their fins. If he could, he would touch them; or hold them – long enough to show them he was their ally, long enough to learn the architecture of their fins. He kept a tray of water in the base of his boat and he would float one or two in this tray while he studied them, while he looked them deep in the eye and their looks fused, trailed off over the high seas like a long conspiratorial ribbon.

To Samuel, the fish were jewels, they were his friends and he loved them. He had no use for them. He did not care for commerce, he did not care to go to the town and trade. Samuel loved them only to hold, only to nurse briefly in his grasp. He would catch one, trembling hands, scrutinise the intricacy of its beauty. He would catch another, read in its colours, in its shape, the long triumphant story of its evolution. He would catch a shoal – perhaps of mackerel or maybe smaller, perhaps of bitterling, and they glimmered in his boat and he always marvelled.

But, above all, it was the ones that would never be caught that held Samuel's interest. To win them from the far deep to the bay; to win them out of the water, to lure them into his net, into the lap of his boat that he could say I have had him, I have known him. To draw them from far off that he might know them, know every single scale, run his fingers over every single wisp and whisker, gill and fin. To let his eyes bask in the glinting colours, the matt-dead grey, the endless kaleidoscopic gleam. To come onto the diamond water, to sit for hours in the smile of the sun, to hear only the wind, the breeze as it whispered in his ears, to be just alone, just him and his skiff, in and out of the rocks, at the edge of the black sands, to dance them out, sing them out, wish them out of the depths, into his arms, into his reed-woven net.

Then to drop them back as God would have wished, trail them softly back into the water, whisper to their departing sheen be safe, be quick . . .

Until he died, no one joined Samuel on his beach. People stayed away from him. They thought he was possessed. He wore his black hat, black cloak come hail or shine, never smiled, smoked on his pipe, growled plenty, spoke little. People said he was evil or bad or worse. They blamed him when their lambs died or their apple crop failed. They brought curses down on his name every time a problem came whose source they could not, or would not, fathom. They feared him. They feared his independence, his incredible determination. They feared the way he did not need them, did not need the company of men but could overcome insurmountable obstacles single-handed.

But Samuel took no notice of all this. Samuel did not see their fear or heed their superstition. He did not hear the words that they used when they spoke of him – strange, wild, dangerous, hermity. Samuel was safe in his hut on his beach. He did not care for the town or for its inhabitants. He was a poet of the land, poet of the sea. He lured fish to the bay that would otherwise have never been seen and in his time, the waters there grew even more fecund, even more rich with life. He carved designs in the wood that only an artist could conceive. He sang tunes on the winds, his voice like that of a woman, so that in time a legend grew up about a mermaid who lived on the Deadmen.

For many years, fifty at least, Samuel remained in his blood-red hut. Remote, alone, driven, he was an unlikely hero – yet Samuel for those fifty years was a mean custodian of those magical waters.

And then at last his vigil came to an end. Astride his boat, net in hand, cloak draped over the bench like a flag. Samuel was old now, maybe seventy. His cheeks were puckered with lines and his teeth were few and stumpy. On the sea, if you had seen him, you might have thought him blind also because you could not see his eyes, they were screwed tight and his lids drooped low in thick unmoving curtains.

Samuel felt a pain. It went through his eye, through the heart of his face, tore down his arm. He knew that the gods meant him to go now and he sang out, one last elegy to this place that he had nurtured all these years, one last song to the fish, to the rippling embrace of his bay. The pain lingered – it was almost beautiful, danced in his veins like the joy that whistled in his ears during those moments when his toes first felt the softness of the iron-black sand. There was an utter stillness. No wind, no waters swooshing, no slithering of the necklaces of fish. Samuel stood up, facing the blood-red hut and the Lion Rock. And then he looped, like one of his dolphins, into the water. No sound.

It did not take long for the fishermen and all the people in the nearby town to hear that Samuel, guardian of the bay, had died. Somehow they knew. Maybe it was the fish moaning on the winds or the cutty-grass whining long laments. Maybe it was the pain roaring from the Lion Rock as it mourned its departed friend.

Soon they came. At first it was just a few – a couple of men here and there. For hours they fought the battle of the path, cut their way through the overhanging scrub. At times, as the thorn tore at their flesh and the rocks snapped at their feet, they thought they might give up. They cursed the name of Samuel and they would have turned back, they would have abandoned the journey but for the lure of all those fish.

And then at last it was over and Samuel's Bay was manned once more. They moved into his hut. One of them sat on the chair, the others on the table. There was not much here – a few tools, a hat, a bed if you could call it that. They sat around. The wind blew. They were bored. The wind blew and it seemed to them that there would never be a moment when they could venture out without their hair, their eyes, their skin being covered in a stinging black mask. They tinkered with his things, broke his chisel, finished his tobacco, rocked in his chair until its feet broke. Out back, they found his old still and for eleven consecutive days they remained in a drunken stupor, laughing at Samuel's carved overhangs because, in their inebriation, they could not make out the patterns so they laughed to hide their fear.

But then one day the winds died down and they walked out of the hut and they stood in the smile of the bay and they saw what it was that they had known, what it was that Samuel had been protecting all those years – they saw those thousands and millions of fish, swarming in the waters like nuggets of gold, like lumps of coral, like rocks of unhewn diamond so large that you could not fit them into the palm of your hand. The men stepped into the foremost shallows and their legs were bombarded by the tickling of the fins. They scrambled their way up the sheer sides of the Lion Rock and saw the gentle lightning, the necklaces upon necklaces of fish. They rolled their heads back on their shoulders and heard, sure enough, the snaking of all those fins. It was a miracle. The townsmen laughed. They looked at each other and they sat down in the waters with the fish colliding with their calves and they laughed until they were as drunk on greed as they had been on Samuel's home-made Scotch.

They made a boat – like Samuel, using driftwood from the last victim of the Deadmen – hurriedly and it was leaky but it did not matter because they had to get out there, they had to pull them in, rake them in. Like thieves in a cave filled with treasure, they raided the sea. Saliva ran down their chins, their eyes glistened. They filled the boat until there was barely enough room to stand. Then they filled it some more and swam back, pulling the boat as they went. The fish swilled over the sides for the boat was almost submerged. They brought it up onto the sand, the veins bursting in their foreheads. And they tipped the fish out onto the beach and ran their fingers through them, slipping them through as a diamond dealer might through hundreds and thousands of uncut gems.

Day in, day out, they continued their rape of the sea. It became an addiction, not the eating of the fish, not the poetry of the water but just the getting of them, the taking of them. Day in, day out, their boat groaning under its load. They made a second boat, then a third. More men came from the town. They too built boats and soon the path to Samuel's Bay was well trodden and the waters covered in craft of every imaginable shape and size. They fished, every one of them, without thought. They invented more ways of taking them, not just nets or lines but nets and lines and crates. At night their candle lanterns looked like fireflies bobbing up and down in the wind.

Imagine you are suspended in a desert with no water for several days – then suddenly you find a lake. You are afraid that it is or might become a mirage so you fill every canister you can find with water, every sock, every glove. You do not seem to care that the sock cannot hold its load, that the glove soon becomes lost in the sand. Greed, lust, relief, basic human idiocy take over.

So it was with those first fishermen who came to Samuel's Bay in the wake of his death. They would take catches larger than they could manage, reeling in tons of fish for the naked, throaty pleasure of seeing them captured by their own hand. Piles of them would lie dead on the sand because the barrows which the fishermen had brought from the town were not large enough. For those first few years after his death, Samuel's Bay became known not only for the hut, for the Lion Rock, for the narrow frightening path but also for the stink of fish rotting pointlessly along the back of the beach.

Soon enough the blood-red hut was no longer sufficiently large to house all the fishermen who wished to take their chances in the shadow of the Lion Rock. Soon enough the men grew tired of rolling on top of one other each night and gradually they did as Samuel had done, took driftwood from the sands, built huts of their own. They too added tin roofs and chimney stacks from the litter they gathered along the shore. For ease of distinction, each man painted his hut a different colour. They brought their wives, their families. Samuel's Bay became home to a village. If you fought your way down the path, you would hear the sound of voices – children playing in the dunes, women hanging their clothes to dry on the flax bushes. A hammer might be banging, one man might be shouting to another.

Years went on and at last the waters of Samuel's Bay began to show signs of the heartless ravaging that had taken place day in, day out since the old man's death. Now you could not smell the rotting fish because the fishermen had finally realised they must be thrifty. They no longer dropped piles of them on the sand. Indeed, now they were lucky to find enough to fill one barrow between two boats. You went and stood up on the Lion Rock and the necklaces were fewer and further between. Something of the gleam went out of the waters. The air of excitement that had once filled this huge cove had died.

Yet this inevitable dropping-off of the fish did not deter the fishermen. Still they went on fishing as long as the hours would allow. Hurl out the nets, sling out the lines, pile the fish high in the keel. No thought for the preservation of their livelihoods, no thought for their sons or their sons' sons who, needs must, would be dependent on these waters to feed their kin. It was a wretched downward spiral of avarice and destruction. They fished the waters until there was not one single shoal left to reel in. They trawled the bottom of that sorry bay until all they brought in were stones, until all you could see in the water was the glinting of old Samuel's eyes as he flashed out his displeasure . . .

Dublin Small is growing old. He aches when he stands and he aches when he sits and there are moments too when he aches even lying down in bed. Nowadays, when he removes his cap to wipe back his hair, he finds nothing – only slick, naked scalp. When he spends time on his chair on the beach – which he has done every afternoon since he can remember – Dublin can find that hours go by and he does not recall what has taken place.

Old as he is, Dublin Small believes there is nothing new that he has not seen. There are no fish he has not caught, no flowers he has not studied and sniffed and pressed dry in his book. There are no sensations he has not felt – wind on his brow, sand in his eyes, in his hair, in his mouth, salt at the back of his throat, triumph, despair, elation, loss. Everything that the gods have had in their basket, they have revealed in Samuel's Bay – so Dublin believes – and since the old man has lived only here, he is sure he will go to his grave having lived a full and vivid life.

But yesterday Dublin saw something the like of which he had never seen before. Dublin goes over the picture of the day in his mind: he sees himself sitting there, waiting for the two Johnnies, wiping the black crust of sand that has stuck to his upper lip. He sees himself as he lights a cheroot and the smoke blows back in his eyes so Dublin is weeping also, from the smoke and the wind, and he curses because it's just bloody typical. Impatient, Dublin scuffs the sand with his feet. He draws the outline of a fish, he begins to hum an old sea-shanty, he looks round again for the twins because Lord knows it's time enough, he blows out more smoke and then he hears a sound and it cuts through the fog of his old-man deafness – and for some reason, Dublin sees at once that he is about to add one more extraordinary experience to his repertoire.

Now it is dawn, the storm has blown over and old man Dublin is cursing again. He has sand in his hair, in his teeth, in his socks, down his shirt. He is surrounded by fish – they have smashed against his windows and battered his chimney – and he is soaked to the skin and freezing too because that wind was bitter it was, and his chair is broken now and still they are not here, still there is no sign of the two Johnnies.

Dublin casts his gaze round the beach, looking for them. He starts to walk and he has to wade ankle-deep through fish. He huffs and puffs because his hips are creaking like old doors. He sucks through his teeth trying to dislodge the grains of sand still wedged between them. Dublin walks down to the end of the bay and he climbs up through the bulbous trees, his hand over his eyes so he can scan the rocks. He goes deep into the barley-sugar cave, he goes up through the cutty-grass, he goes in and out of the huts that still remain and he has to ease aside the odd boat, he has to pick through pieces of wood and piles of debris and a piece of stone here or a lump of coral there.

Exhausted and uncertain where else to look, Dublin hobbles his way back through the wet sand. By some mercy, though the doors have gone and the windows are smeared with fish scales, his hut has survived intact. Dublin sits down on the edge of the veranda. He relights the cheroot that was extinguished by a flying snapper and he watches his breath and the smoke as they swirl on the chill air and he counts the few huts that remain, the dark green one and that yellow one in the corner and the oldest of them all, the red one that was once set back into the dunes, now upturned next to his.

And at last he sees the silhouettes of two old men, walking together as they have always, and Dublin heaves a sigh of relief because hell what a god-almighty-day-and-night it's been.

Athene Brown comes to. She is lying in the middle of the beach, she is surrounded and covered by debris, she is clinging on to an empty chair. In her mouth, Athene tastes the salt-tinny-sweetness of his blood. There is something on her teeth and she wipes it off on the back of her hand and years later she wonders whether that would be the last she ever felt of him, a tiny corner of his skin which she had torn off when she bit into his shin.

Where is she? Athene Brown is only seven and she is assailed once more by the fear that she felt at the height of the storm. Where are the other children? Where are the women, the mothers, where are the boats, where is her hut, where is Isaiah? Athene Brown struggles to stand up but it is hard, the sand is wet. She wants to cry out but her mouth is dry, her lips are dry, there is no moisture, only tears that bump out, bouncing down her cheek like pebbles.

Now she starts to shiver. Now she feels the cold that came with the storm, that throughout the night has been seeping into her. Images flock back into her mind – of the storm and all its frenzy – but consciousness is elusive as water and Athene's vision is coming and going, her mind is fevered, she wants her father, she needs her father.

No one knows she is here. No one in the village – and there are few enough remaining – has a care to look around and find her or anyone who may have survived. Frank Armstrong and Ivy Peacock, the Cuckeltys, the Normans are packing. That was the last straw, the last bloody straw. For years the fish have been dwindling, for years it has been a struggle to live here, to survive here. They have put up with the wind, they have put up with the sand in their hair, their clothes, their eyes, they have put up with the sun which beats down most days hard and hot. They have forgotten how it was, in the good days, how their lives were good and they were lazy, sitting around on chairs, reaping in huge harvests, coming back from the town laden with money.

They have forgotten how they did not save it, they spent it, they bought clothes and boots and wine and meat and mirrors and spices and curtains made of silk and they never saw that they should preserve this life, protect this life.

Admittedly Frank Armstrong and Ivy Peacock and the rest have lasted longer than most. They have been more generous than those others, they have stayed on, lived frugally, shown the bay and its implacable gods some modicum of respect. They have sat in the middle chasing the shadows, playing boules with Dublin or the two Johnnies. They have mended their huts and eaten what they had to and fished in a rota and bowed to the rains.

But now they want to follow the others because the storm was the last bloody straw it was. The town beckons. The town with its warehouses and its factories and its work and its no wind and no sand. Ivy Peacock is running over the dunes, trying to rescue what she can find of her clothes. Frank Armstrong is digging – like a madman – with a shovel, hoping he can uncover his box with all his tools because he has heard from the others who went before him that the town is short of craftsmen. The Cuckeltys and the Normans, they are all at it, scrabbling about on hands and knees, no thought for what they are leaving, no hint of sorrow, only relief because at last, soon, it will be all bloody over.

Isaiah climbs the Lion Rock that towers over the middle of Samuel's Bay. All around, beneath the Lion, there are signs that a terrible punishment has been visited on the bay. Pieces of tin from the roofs of the huts, chimneys folded in two. Sand has spiralled into cones and the twisting winds have altered the line of the beach, the shape of the dunes. They have picked up seaweed and wood; they have picked up stones and sometimes a conch shell or a colony of green-lipped mussels. They have moved in serpentines, capricious; they have danced in and out of the flax bushes, lifted trees from their fragile hold in the soil, taken up tussocks of grass and even, here and there, a hut, a home. Not only that but fish, everywhere – lying dead, lying bruised and broken, lying in heaps, and some, by some cruel stroke, have been kept alive by the numbers of fish that surround them so that every now and again a pile of them flutters, struggles, pushed by one beneath them that is battling with life and death in equal measure.

Isaiah stands motionless, cut out against the mauve stretch of the waters, the azure spread of the sky. He does not look down, only stares directly out to sea. Stand close and you can hear the beating of his heart. Stand in front and you can see the intentness of his gaze, the fierce determination in his chin. Stand as he stands and you feel the yearning in him, the anxiety. What is he doing? You might almost think he was preparing to dive in, for his arms, his head, his whole body are leaning out, stretching out in the upward parabolic curve of a fountain.

No one sees Isaiah. The rim of the wind has singed past the bay, roared through the night, disappeared into the sea. Now day is dawning and the light is curious, half dark, half bright. The bloated golden orb of the sun does nothing, neither burns away the mist nor hides behind the cloud – only it hangs silent and there is no wind and the iron-black sand lies flat. Isaiah does not look down, he does not count the fish or look for his hut or look even for his daughter. He does not smell the smell – scent of charred wood, of things that have burnt because there was a fire and it tore down the beach, stolen by the wind from a stove – for Isaiah is intent on his purpose. In a moment you will see him tense his muscles. In a moment you will hear him draw in his breath. He will lean down further so that his fingertips are level with his knees. He will stick his hips out behind, he will keep his legs, his arms close together as if bound, he will have his head down and his eyes closed . . .

. . . in a moment, the sun will seem to blink, the still winds to gasp – and you will watch aghast as the thin brown body takes its place among the biting cold waters, among the lace-fringed waves that thrash beneath.

Does Isaiah mean to jump? Or to dive? Does he mean to fall, to hurl himself into the sea with no care? Or is he diving out, over the Lion's paws, to swim through the deep waters beyond? Isaiah himself could not answer the question. He leaves the top of the Lion Rock, arcs out like a falling star, and he hits the chill of the water and he is alive, unbroken by the fall. Next he swims, snaking his way through the pull of the waves, negotiating the undertow like a child of the sea, boy whose bones are made from the winnowing reeds, whose blood purrs with the salt and the roar of the iron-black sands.

Isaiah is no longer thinking. He swims because it comes to him as instinct. He swims and he fights the water and he pushes himself on and on, losing himself in the heave, pushing himself so that he does not have to contemplate the demons on his tail. The sun slowly creeps out from within the mist, spreads its scarlet tendrils over the water, and Isaiah finds a rhythm. It is close to the rhythm of his broken heart and he swims on and on, pressing forwards until his muscles can take it no longer, until the weight of his arms and his legs becomes too heavy for him, fit though he is, to endure. He bumps in and out of inlets, in and out of dreams.

Early dawn becomes early morning. The scarlet tendrils have bled into the water and the sun now blazes, the sky shimmering in hot white ribbons. A barge is pushing out onto the coast, with a load of coal and logs, dog on the prow, children lined up on the deck to scan the horizon for rocks, fish, danger. One of the children sees a body afloat in the water. The child cries out Hallooo Hallooo and the bargemaster throws out a rope, pulls the man in. They turn about. They are afraid the man is going to die aboard their barge so they head back up the river, forcing the heavy boat against the current. When at last they can, they drop him off – at the fringes of the town, in the outskirts of the big town and they say there you go now, they say off you go and they pump his chest to force out all the water, then turn back down before the tide goes out again and it is too late for their journey.

The two Johnnies move slowly. Dublin Small cannot see them clearly at first, his eyesight is growing weak and he mutters under his breath because he is angry at all the little secrets old age keeps revealing to him. They inch towards him and Dublin watches them, impatient, he wants to go out and pull them in like a mother, rough and cross and relieved all at once because finally her children have reappeared. Slowly the dim hum of their voices rolls towards him over the devastated beach. Slowly their old-man silhouettes become larger against the dirty-golden-grey backdrop of the horizon. Dublin sits, trying hard to keep his fulminations under control.

But it is no use ... all-those-fish-Lord-be-damned-where've-you-got-to-worried-sick-looked-high-and-low-bloody-idiots-what-were-you-thinking-of ... the words pour out, steam from a kettle, and Dublin feels so rough-cross-relieved, he wants to cuff them so he does, he wants to biff them or something, touch them because for a moment there he thought he had lost them altogether ...

The old men are carrying something. There is a bundle in between them, he could not make out what it was quite but now he can and Dublin shuts up, drops his jaw. He thought they might have died, he thought they might have been blown away by the storm or hit by falling debris or drowned or they might just have flaming died; but of all the blessed things that might have detained them, kept them out of sight so that he could not find them anywhere, not anybloodywhere at all, Dublin Small did not imagine it could be a seven-year-old girl.

They are taking turns to carry her. She is limp like a rag doll and he can see her eyes are closed and at first Dublin is not sure, is she alive or is she dead. The old men twitter. Dublin says they should take her inside but the twins are worried, they think the hut might not be safe, who knows what's going to happen next so they bicker for a while and her eyes seem to open so they talk some more, bombarding her with questions. She does not seem to answer but her lips grow tinged with blue until at last they wrap her in a blanket and Dublin holds her, turning his head to the side so he does not blow the smoke in her eyes.

There are four of them on the veranda, old legs, young legs, tails of blanket dangling. Sit for a while and there's silence because so much has happened. Noisy pictures. Grunts of fatigue, puffs from a dying cheroot and finally they ask her, they say where's Isaiah, where's your father then and she cannot speak, she must be too cold, her eyes are glazed, lips suffused with blue; but at last she speaks. And the old men's eyebrows raised in expectation fall at once because all she can manage is a seven-year-old-girl echo of their question.

Where is Isaiah, where's my father then.

Two

Picture the day when it all began – when Athene Brown sailed into the world, a dark unknowing bundle; when her mother tumbled out, ebbing from life like a wave; when the men from the village came to tell Isaiah they had found a body on the rocks, they were sure it was his father's.

Picture the sun as it glittered on the sea; the sand as it glittered in the sun; the Lion Rock as it viewed the tide of life, rising and falling in the many-coloured huts arrayed across the beach.

Roll back the picture, narrow in the view, watch Isaiah as he paced up and down beside the bed in the blood-red hut that nestled at the back of the dunes. Isaiah holding the hand of his lover; holding her hand as she pushed, as the primeval forces of survival rose up from within, as she cried out – too sharp – and her pain was slowly swallowed by the creeping brown mist of death; holding her hand and at the same time, leaning into her ear, whispering to her, pleading with her, begging her to stay; holding her hand and at the same time, trying to cradle the head of the newborn baby that lay in a rush of fluid between her thighs; holding her hand, begging her to stay, cradling the baby, trying to stifle the wail that bubbled up in his throat because he did not wish to scare the tiny child with the force of his sudden pain.

Then watch Isaiah as he looks up, as shadows fill the door, two heads, grim faces. Watch as his eyes move from their mouths to their eyes, from their eyes to their hands; as he deciphers through one curtain of grief the dreadful glimpse of another; as he takes in a piece of clothing, a broken rudder, a shoe and they all belong to his father and his father should be out, rowing on the sea.

Ezekiel, his father; Comfort, his wife; now Athene Brown, his precious, worshipped daughter. Isaiah remembered that day because who could ever forget such a time. He would dig his nails deep into his palms and still, even up until his dying moments, he could feel the nausea of his pain as it welled inside his throat. He had to lay out his wife, wipe her, wash her, close her stricken eyes. He had to pick up the baby, wrap her in his arms, hold her to the light, summon up that deep surge of love that would not leave him ever. And later that day he had to carry his father's body – old, worn out but heavy none the less – to the top of the Lion Rock, then watch, from the shore, as the flames carried the old fisherman's ashes out over the dark sea.

The gods played with Isaiah. They brought him hope and they took away all joy. They brought him a longed-for, yearned-for child – and they took away a lover he adored and a father whose every move the boy had copied for as far back as he could remember. Isaiah was forced to weigh up the triumph of new life against the tragedy of sudden loss. All in one day he had to become an orphan, a widow, a father, a man.

The tide of life rose and Athene Brown was born. The tide of life fell and Comfort and Ezekiel were taken away. Isaiah, man-boy, stood in the middle, looked down at his daughter, wondered what on earth he was to do.

Sometimes years later, when he struggled to survive and the bay withheld its treasures, Isaiah cursed the bond he had enjoyed with his papa. Maybe, if they had not been so close, Isaiah would have learnt more? Maybe, if Isaiah had fought with his father, resisted the old man, he would have been allowed to participate more fully in his own survival?

For throughout Isaiah's childhood, throughout his teen years and even up until the day Ezekiel died, Isaiah's father had sought to keep his son sheltered from the matter of life. If there were fish to catch, it was Ezekiel who went alone to work the seas. If there were voyages to make, trips to the town, to the market to be made, repairs to be carried out, it was always Ezekiel who executed them.

Perhaps, at times, he would allow the boy to help him scrape the molluscs off the boat's bottom. Perhaps he would take Isaiah down between the claws of the Lion's feet and together they would count the shrimp or watch the green-lipped mussels as they clung to the rocks, waving in the tide. If the sun shone, Ezekiel might take his son to the top of the great rock and point out – with his old trembly hands – those stretches of the water to avoid and those to frequent; in the evenings, they might sit in the barley-sugar cave or up among the cutty-grass, and Ezekiel would talk to his boy about the legend of Samuel, about the types of fish and the types of sea-bird and the signs to follow and the warnings to heed.

But when the old man died, when Isaiah stood that day, shadows in the door, when he looked down at the child in his arms, at this tiny mouth opening and closing, Isaiah knew for certain that being taught was quite different from being allowed to learn for yourself; that experience was as precious and fleeting as water; that he knew nothing – not about the bay, not about surviving, not about loss or grief or caring for others; in short, that his father had taught him little that equipped him for the terrible situation he now faced.

Not only that but at the age of eighteen, when he should have been easing his father aside, insisting on learning his trade, Isaiah fell in love – he met Comfort.

Comfort with her trail of feathers and her silvery veils and her sequins and the coloured pebbles and they all came in a cloud, as she did, from nowhere Isaiah had ever seen before. Comfort from the city, who arrived one day at the bay, nobody could be sure how or why, who walked into Isaiah's light as he looked out over the sea keeping watch for his father, and said can you show me the way back to the ridge please. Comfort who seduced him even with those words because she was so young, because she was winsome and graceful, because she put her hand to her lip and touched it – gently – with her finger, then looked away so he could run his gorging eyes down the full length of her profile.

Years later Isaiah had asked himself whether they knew perhaps that they did not have long. Was there some sense in the air which said you must love her now, you must love her true and strong and passionate because it may not last? Isaiah took his Comfort and they ran the length of the bay. He showed her the barley-sugar cave with its sand-striped roof, he showed her the space in the cutty-grass and the long fat trees where you could hide and the best way to climb the Lion and the channels in the rocks where the agapanthus grew. He kissed her eyes and he kissed her back and he kissed all the coloured stones that fell out of her bag and together they rolled in the sand until they became one, until you could not tell them apart.

Once he asked Ezekiel if they could go out with him – if they could sail in the boat so the old man could show her the glory of their sea – but they did not mind when he refused because there were only seconds, moments left to them. Once Isaiah asked will you take me over the ridge, will you show me your place and they walked up, through the trees and the scrub, in and out of the orchards and fields, along an old path and they stood on top of a hillock at the edge of a yawning plain while she pointed out, in the far distance, the rows of crooked chimney-tops that marked out her city – but it was taking too long, they were walking when they should be close, entwined, drawing pictures of one another interlocked in the sand – and soon Isaiah said he had seen enough and they turned round.

And then she was pregnant and Isaiah was so filled with love for her and life and himself, his blessed self, that Isaiah forgot all notion of the present. He did not notice what otherwise for sure he would have seen – how his father was ageing visibly; how the boat was going out for longer, bringing less and less in each time it returned; how the words that Ezekiel had to share with his son were jumbling up, gushing out in angry spits; how their hut grew an empty feel and the village too, because now it was difficult for them all, now the smell of city riches lured them back.

Isaiah told his daughter nothing of this. She knew nothing of the pain of Isaiah's double loss. She was too young, how could he have told her what it had been like, to sit one moment and watch his wife as she died in childbirth, then to hear at another that his father – who knew the sea as well as any of them – had been washed up in tatters and fragments at the feet of the Lion Rock.

Isaiah told her only of the love that they had shared. He told her – as she grew from a child to a girl and her mind opened like a flower – of Comfort, his birdoflove. He pointed out the chimes she had made – of cuttlefish and shells, leaves of mica and pieces of glass; how she had hung them in their hut and they rang, then and always, with the sound of the sea. Isaiah would sit in his old rocker – the one they had found on the veranda that must have belonged to Samuel – with his tiny girl wrapped in his knees and there they were with the lilac-blue stretching out before them, a hundred precious stories hanging in the air. He drew her pictures of those magical months when he had been in love. He told her and she believed him always that Comfort had died with words of love on her lips, with a beatific smile. He described her mother to her and Athene Brown carried with her throughout her life a portrait of Comfort, in her mind's eye. Comfort, young. Comfort, pretty, thin. Comfort with her hair long, plaited, then twisted up in a casual soft bump at the back of her head and it bowed down at the sides, slipped out so that there was always a stray lock hanging by her cheek. Comfort making things, collecting things, decking out their hut so that it was still sparse and small but it was home with pieces of mirror and patches of multi-patterned cloth and shells and coloured stones perched on ledges, hanging in rows from strings. And there was always a painted chair and a flaky-painted table, there was always cotton on the bed and curtains on the window and an old glass bowl which must have come from a ship and which she had hung from the ceiling upside down so that they could fill it with candles and sit there in the evenings with the ring of the chimes and the light's flickering patterns jumping in and out of the salty-wooden walls.

Athene Brown remembered those years with her father and it had been a brilliant voyage through a bright garden. She remembered his breath – when he held her close. She remembered his eyes – when he held her close and he looked at her and she could see in them, for all their sadness, how very much he loved her. She remembered he had made her a boat, she recalled he had shown her flowers and insects, creatures and their tiny habitats and she had walked with him, learnt to speak with him, learnt all the lessons that a man could teach whose bones were made from the winnowing reeds, whose blood purred with the salt from the sea.

Sometimes she thought she could recall the families who had been there – the women, bending over, washing bottoms, the children always covered in a fine layer of sand, always dark from the sun, burnt from the wind. There were days when the men from the village played boules – chasing the shade so they did not remain exposed to the glare of the sun and Athene Brown felt sure there were crowds of them, Isaiah among them taking his turn. The men spat and the children chased one another through the shallows and the wind blew and the sand stung your ankles. There was the Carnival of the Fish, when the young men fought and there were flags and bunting and jugs of cider made from the apples that hung in the orchards up on the ridge. She thought she could recall that last carnival and it was as it should have been – the young men of the village lined up in rows, glinting in the sun, going out in their boats and fighting all day with the marlin, pulling and leaning against the weight of fish who were fearsome, relentless battlers, who would not go to their deaths unless the fight was well and truly lost.

Some days in particular – Athene's birthday when she was six – and Isaiah woke her early for the sun was cool then and there was no wind and she put her hand in his and they set out, sucked into the dry sand, buoyed up by the wet. She remembered looking up at him and his profile was always the same. She remembered breathing in, the air was fresh and she smelt his smell – fox and salt and wind. She remembered asking him where are we going Papa and he turned down to her, smiled into her, said nothing. They walked through the rocks – above the dunes

36

but below the ridge because there the agapanthus grew most abundantly – and they staggered down with armfuls of blue flowers which they draped along the edge of their boat in festoons. They walked to the ridge and picked fruit, plums and apples, peaches and lemons and they brought them down, staggering, giggling. They picked up a blanket here and a basket there, a bottle of elderberry wine and a knife and Isaiah was singing, he was smiling, he was laughing.

And then they set sail – before the sun was too high – little boat groaning under its load and they made for the island far to the west of Samuel's Bay. Athene at the prow, Isaiah at the helm, the blood-red ketch bobbing up and down in the waves and then it grew too hot so Athene sat in the cabin and counted out the bread that they would eat or the sprats that they would use to catch the snapper or the cups that they needed and the plates. Isaiah looking up and out over the horizon. Isaiah steering, serious, the sail swinging back and forth and he would shout out, every now and again, mind your head mind your head and in her dreams it would sing out over the waves like a hymn, hymn of the sea.

And all that day the sun not fierce but kind so that it danced in the catspaws and it caught every now and again on a small shoal of fish or the belly of a minke because there was a family of whales that had been coming here for years, and there would be a flash which splintered into a hundred flashes, gleaming against the side of the boat like jewels.

And just as the sun was not strong, so the wind was weak, Isaiah almost had to row at some points, and they took all day to reach this island which they wanted to explore, it was said there were huge stocks of mussels on the far side. So they pitched camp on the beach, sitting in the shade of a sail which Isaiah had rooted into the sand, flames of a bonfire crackling at their feet. Athene Brown could recall the fish that she had caught earlier on the boat, how she had run along the planks shouting Papa Papa and he came and together they pulled it in, laid it out on the deck, inspected it. And later that night, when the sun was easing down behind them, cooking it over flames in the sand and there was the rich deep odour of leaves burning, fish cooking, lips smacking.

How many times did they leave Samuel's Bay? Athene Brown looked back and she remembered only that time when they went to the island, when they trawled the rocks for mussels and they found no such thing, only new shells and new sand, new sea and a new kind of wind and a view of Samuel's Bay and the Lion and the white waters around the Deadmen that she would never forget. They rarely left and as she saw it, from all those years and all those miles beyond, they did not need to. They had food there and shelter there, space there and time there, they had love there – as she saw it – real love, they were two and their loves were interconnecting, enmeshed as a perfect unit, undying.

And when she looked back on her early childhood, when she tried to rediscover all it was that she lost so young, Athene Brown thought too she could recall the days of plenty. She imagined the fish dropping from the barrows because the boats had come in so full. She imagined the fishermen and their wives smiling – an everlasting smile of prosperity – because life was so good, the seas were so kind. She persuaded herself that the fish-storm was one of many; that it was inevitable that sudden twisting winds should throw up fish, there were so many of them teeming in the lilac-blue waters. She saw the flags bobbing in the everlasting winds, she saw the black sand glittering between a sandwich of mauve-tinged sea and endless amethyst sky. She saw her father cut out in profile, atop the Lion, his hand to his forehead and she knew he was looking out across shoals of fish and all he need do was choose his moment.

She could paint a picture of the sky, of the ocean, of the tiny huts tucked in between. She could draw if she was asked a day or a week or a year during those times because they lived with her always, they did not leave her, they flowed through her dreams. And the days, weeks, years always sounded in her mind the same, chiming to the ring of the cuttlefish and the music of the sea as it blew through the veranda. She recalled those first seven years – when they were together, man and daughter, man and shadow – and she recalled his smile, when he looked at her, when he picked her up, when they walked out over the rocks together, small girl, tall man, and perhaps she confused in her mind the love she had known from him and she had cast it wider, over the bay, over the sea so that the waters teemed then as they had for Samuel. She reasoned that Isaiah had left her not because he had wanted to but because of the storm, because it sucked him away. She spent her childhood with Dublin Small, with the two Johnnies and she was not sad, only grateful. She missed him but she rejoiced: everything had been good, she had not been punished, only granted a glimpse of something sublime.

Three

And just as Athene Brown recalled those years and she saw them only as precious, only as golden, so Isaiah lived them, ignoring his grief for his birdoflove, burying himself instead in love for his daughter.

Every waking thought he filled with pictures of her. She cried and he jumped. She laughed and his heart leapt. He might take a blanket and prop her up in the hull of his boat while he scratched at it, banged at it and she would gurgle, grant him a smile. He might bind her to his back with a scarf or two and he would march perhaps up over the ridge, through the woods part wild, part tame and he would pick a fruit and let her try to grasp it, watch as her fingers grappled with the mystery of holding and the mystery of life. Or sometimes, when the wind was flat and the sea was flat, they might swim together and Isaiah lay on his back with his neck resting in the water while she floated on his stomach, while the sea crept into her bones, became one with her blood.

And as she grew, he took her for walks – the ones she recalled all those years later – up along the ridge, down along the beach, sometimes even to the tip of the Lion's nose. They skirted in and out of the rocks to pick flowers. They walked in and out of the velvet pools between the claws of the Lion searching for sea anemones, soft like blooms. He showed her plants, he showed her wildlife and explained the ways that this insect or that mammal worked. She asked a question and he would rack his brains for an answer that would leave her face filled with a smile. He explained to her the essence of nature as he understood it and for all that she was only young, Athene Brown absorbed these lessons, kept them close to her heart for scores of years to come. He made her a boat, a miniature replica of the one that his father had made him – and sometimes, on special occasions and when the wind was not too fierce, they sailed out together, big boat, little boat, big man, little girl. At nights, when she slept, when his love was at its height, Isaiah would steal in from the veranda and watch her – in her basket, in her cot, in the tiny bed he had made on his woodbench – whisper in her dreaming ears the prayers of the stars and the hymn of the rains and his breath was warm – as he bent down beside her, as he leant into the curl of her sleep – and sometimes Isaiah thought he only breathed so that he could smell the small-girl perfume of her hair.

Perhaps he was blinded by love. Perhaps he was blinded by the love he had just experienced with Comfort and the love he was now feeling with Athene Brown. Perhaps he was dazzled by the bright white sea and the hot sun and the importance he felt each time he geared up the sails and set out across the bay because now he was a man, now he had a role to fulfil. Perhaps, each time he came back in from a day on the water, when she was cared for by Ivy Peacock or Mrs Cuckelty, and he had nothing to show for it, Isaiah was not perturbed because joy at the prospect of seeing her eclipsed everything, everything else. Perhaps it was difficult for Isaiah – who for so long had been a boy – to become a man, to be able to absorb disappointment, then examine it, then accept it, then act on it.

Dancing in the waters of love, Isaiah rowed out. He could spend all day and catch nothing; he could spend all day and catch one fish or one crab. Dancing in the waters of love, Isaiah rowed far and wide and he barely caught enough to sustain even himself.

In truth, if Isaiah ever stopped to reflect, he would have seen that he did not know Samuel's Bay. Of course he had been out in the boat; of course he had fished a little, sailed a little. Of course they had swum there, lived there, breathed the salt of the sea, the blow of the winds. And for sure, Isaiah had lived only there.

But he and his father, they were like the sun and its shadow. They looked and breathed and felt with the same eyes, same lungs, same heart. They were man-and-boy and they walked together or sat together or Isaiah listened while Ezekiel told him stories or Isaiah sat while Ezekiel rowed or Isaiah ate while Ezekiel provided the food.

And Isaiah never looked for himself or saw for himself. His father worked and for the most part he kept Isaiah safe at home. His father fished and Isaiah did not want for anything.

*   *   *

But slowly it began to dawn on Isaiah. Slowly he began to realise how little he knew about the sea around Samuel's Bay. He went out every day in his boat and came back with nothing or maybe a sprat or two or maybe a crab. He went out at dawn, at midday, at dusk and he moved this way and that, feeling his way round the rocks and the inlets but still it did not help him, whether he changed his habits, whether he followed this route or that.

He saw those last remaining fishermen now in a way he had never seen them before, and they sat around, their bellies sprawling over their trousers as enforced idleness seeped through their bones. Their faces were slack, their eyes drooped, they seemed to spend all day not out fishing but lounging in their beds; or they were not mending their boats but draped over rickety chairs, spitting a bit on the sand, grunting about how bad things were.

Isaiah saw men whose names were dim echoes from his childhood – Ron Cuckelty, the two Johnnies, Frank Armstrong – and he saw families whose sons perhaps he might have played with but more likely he was told by his father to avoid and they were all tattered, they were all struggling, you could tell from their clothes if you chose to look, from the way their coloured huts no longer gleamed as they once had.

Isaiah decided he would push out further. He was young he thought he was strong he thought he was keen-eyed and needy where all the rest of them were old and resigned. He reasoned that if Ezekiel had made it work, so could he. He reasoned furthermore that he did not have a choice, that the gods could not be so cruel, that there was a child to feed, a child to clothe and if he did not succeed in that, what point was there to his existence?

So he planned a long trip. He filled his boat with lines and nets, with bait and buckets. He stacked fruit in the hold and logs for a fire and some clothes and a knife and he gave Athene to Ivy Peacock and he said I will be back in a week, maybe two. And he left, sure in his heart that he would come back triumphant.

Isaiah pushed out to sea beneath the turquoise cup of the sky. He weaved round the Deadmen and he sailed until there was nothing to see but water, nothing to hear but the wail of the gulls and the howl of the hot sea-wind. He sailed for a night and then another. He thought the waters here must be rich, he thought I know I can win where those other men have failed, he thought he did not want to accept that he had made a mistake in trusting his fate to Samuel's Bay.

Isaiah rowed and sailed until he was all but afraid that he might not find his way back home. He followed currents, he watched the winds, he tried to listen to the drift of the tides. He followed trails of water and he looked out for long strips of seaweed and when at last he felt that he had a few of the correct ingredients in place, he dropped anchor, tossed out a line here, laid a net there. And he lit up his pipe. And he waited.

But they did not come. All that day, all the next, for two days three days four, Isaiah remained in the deep waters. He wore a hat, an old dark brown fedora which must have belonged to Samuel himself, and he peered out from beneath the velvety rim hoping upon hope that his fear was unjustified, that his nagging doubts were ready to be banished.

And he had so much to prove, Isaiah. To himself, to the old men who sat and spat, to his little girl whom he adored. He had to prove he could do it, be a man. Proud of Ezekiel, he had to show to his father's ghost that he had earned this right – to fish here, live here. He had to show to the ghost of Samuel that the men before him had not spoilt the place; he had to show to the memory of Comfort that it was not in vain, her death, that Athene would have a good, a better life; he had to find fish, catch fish, because what else was he if not a fisherman and where else would he survive if not here?

Isaiah took the boat further out than he had ever been before. He went to waters deeper than he had ever seen, weathered storms fiercer than he thought possible. He ran in and out of rocks, through channels, across wide straits of sapphire. He stayed out for four, then five nights, then ten, twelve days in a row. He went over the places he had already visited a hundred times, eyes reddening with the strain of scouring the waters. He called out, he sang out as he knew old Samuel had before him and his voice became frail, his arms turned soft with exhaustion, his body grew thin from lack of food and sleep.

That night, the night of his return from his fruitless trawl of the sea, Isaiah thought he would never forgive himself for having been such a fool. He dragged his boat in through the shallows. He was half dressed, worn to a pile of bones, eyes closing with fatigue, hat shoved down on his head like a helmet.

Isaiah went to talk to Dublin Small. He did not run to his daughter or push himself up the sands to the red hut that nestled at the back of the dunes because Isaiah was too ashamed. He said to Dublin you knew all along. He said you knew all along. And he said and how long has it been this way. And Isaiah saw, from the shrug of the old man's shoulders, from the pause that preceded his speech and the deep grooves of his eyes, that he was right, that they had known all along, that the Carnival of the Fish was a sham, that the bay had been empty for years.

So now Isaiah is no longer a boy, he is a man. He sees he has made a mistake that will haunt him until his dying day and this, overnight, has added a decade to his face. Isaiah trudges back to the blood-red hut, bends down to avoid knocking the chimes, nods meekly at Ivy Peacock who has been growing worried he's been away so long, then smiles because she looks alarmed, flops down in the old rocker outside, sucks on his pipe. Does not even kiss his daughter.

After that life in Samuel's Bay was never the same for Isaiah. A chink of light had been stolen from his heart.

Isaiah whiled hours away in the rocker and he thought of his father. He thought of the breadth of his shoulders, the straight tall strut of his back. He thought of his wisdom, his pride, his stubbornness. With a rush, back flowed all that pain. Isaiah did not wish to grow up. He saw how it was to be a father. He thought of the secrets that parents must keep from their children, of the secrets that a man must keep from his family. He saw how Ezekiel had kept so many secrets from his son – the truth of the empty waters, the truth of their struggle to survive. He had allowed Isaiah to grow attached to a place that could never possibly sustain him. He had allowed his dreams and his heart to be filled with a story that was not true. What was Samuel in fact but a legend? What was the beauty of nature except a mirage?

Isaiah rocked in his rocker, tapped lugubriously at his pipe, chipped at pieces of wood on his sawhorse. He was disappointed, bitterly so. He began to look back on his childhood as little more than an exercise in folly. Ezekiel had protected him because he loved him, no doubt, but perhaps it was true also that he had protected him because he wished to protect himself. He could not face, as a father, seeing the pain of a son who was already motherless. He did not wish to tear him away from a place where his roots were so deeply entrenched and so he nurtured him in the solace of a lie.

Isaiah had no one with whom to share his disappointment. He could not speak to the old men because there was nothing new they could say. He could not speak to his father because still he was too hurt, too filled with rage and he was afraid of shouting at the ghost of someone he had loved.

Sometimes at night, when Athene slept next door and the red hut breathed silent in the rhythm of her sleep, he tried to speak to Comfort. He would roll over in his cotton bed and bury his nose in the back of his birdoflove, he would run his fingers over the mound of her hips, he would dance his ankles round hers and he would try to remake the joy that they had known, that he had felt in those early years.

He spoke to her in whispers, in poems whose words danced like feathers and he saw her face again, tress of hair dropping by her cheek, trails of ribbons waltzing by her side ...

... but nights were dreams and in the morning Isaiah found the words still lying on his pillow, empty packets.

There was a torpor that Isaiah felt seep through him and it became increasingly pernicious. They had a shed, they had some curtains, what else did they need in fact? What was ambition and energy and drive if all you needed was an illusion? Athene Brown looked back on those years as the only times, the precious only times. She knew nothing of how it had really been.

You might say that Isaiah was cruel as Ezekiel had also been cruel. You might say that he paved a street with gold when all there was was iron-black sand. Father begat father and they were each, for their separate reasons, afraid to endanger the brittle bonds that held them to their children. They saw, each father, a vulnerability in the next generation which they felt compelled to shield; and they saw also their own vulnerability, mirrored and equalled, and then they were afraid.

Seven years ebbed and the torpor all but paralysed Isaiah. His limbs grew heavy as his heart. The weight of his secret grew each day harder to bear. There were fewer and fewer fish, it was more and more difficult to survive. Sometimes they would go together on outings. To pick fruit (because they had to), to walk up over the ridge and gather anything they could bottle and preserve. To scan the beach for booty because every now and then an item of value might be washed up and Isaiah could hide it in his trousers, then take it to the town to exchange for something they needed. To that far island where they had been told there were plenty of mussels – only they were not the first, the two Johnnies had been there months before and now there was no such thing, only endless sky and endless wind.

Sometimes he would just sit – Athene Brown on his lap, the huge sweep of the bay laid out before him. Samuel's dark brown fedora on his head because that made him feel safer, that made him secure in the truth of the legend. And he would look out, clinging on to her, over the bright sea.

Four

Could anyone have understood just what pitch of disappointment and despair Isaiah had reached? Could anyone have prevented what happened on that morning after the fish-storm? Years later Athene Brown kicked over the ashes of that day, trying to understand, but she had been so young, the truth was obscure and if she looked too close, her memories turned to water.

Perhaps it was true that Isaiah's strength, his hope, his will to live had all but disappeared. Perhaps it was true that he woke that morning and the frail threads of his existence depended on his fixing the hole in that boat. Perhaps it was only in the comfort of detail that Isaiah could carry on and so he awoke and he picked up his hammer and his saw and he banged and he hee-hawed. No one – not Ezekiel's ghost, not Athene Brown, not the Lion Rock himself – knew how frail Isaiah was. Not even Isaiah himself realised how fragile he had become in the face of constant, unrelenting frustration.

You might have thought that the beauty of Samuel's Bay could have sustained him; that the love for his daughter who was growing every day more intriguing, more heart-tingling could have buoyed him up; that the ring of the sea-chimes and the nap of the dark brown velvet fedora and the memory of his birdoflove, her soft hips, her dropping hair could have held him – somehow.

But the fish-storm blew up and Isaiah felt himself mocked not just in one way but in several. Thousands and thousands of fish landed at Isaiah's feet at a moment when the family was all but starved, at a point when Isaiah thought he could carry on the pretence no longer. They came in such numbers and in such circumstances that Isaiah and his daughter, they could not enjoy them, eat them, sell them – only they had to sit on a chair in the full glare of the storm and watch as the fish gasped to death, as they were bruised and damaged and battered upon one another, upon the rocks.

And the storm did not stop at that but it picked up Isaiah's boat, flipped it across the bay so that it smashed upon the rocks, and it took his sawhorse and his hammer, his chisel and his nails and Isaiah saw the little things, the detail in which he could hide, wrested from his grasp in the blink of an eye.

And then too the winds picked up the blood-red shanty and they threw the hut across the bay and they sucked up the sea-chimes which Comfort had made and they hurled them out to sea and Isaiah had to watch it – the legend of Samuel destroyed for ever, last emblems of her love washed away.

Isaiah sat on the chair in the middle of the bay with his daughter's fingers wrapped around his purple neck. There seemed nothing left for him to do. He forgot all about

Athene, only he hurtled down the chute of his pain and he could not stop. He closed his eyes and wandered back – to the iron-black sand, to the pits in the face of the Lion, to the curve of the sea, the smile of the bay that he had known when he was a boy. Fish swam in his blood – in the tired dew of his eyes, in the prickling tears that landed on his sea-bronzed lap. Fish whispered to him, fish called him – snapper and grouper, hoki and cod – fish danced on his knees, in and out of his dark-blue toes. He smelt the salt. He saw the blue and the crash, red of the wind, green of the sea. He ran again – through the velvet pools, through the white-hot sand – and his father was there, in his flight, in his hair, in the echo of the wind and the rush of the pounding waters.

Perhaps now, as he rose to go, he saw that he had brought it all on himself; that he had been wrong to embark on any of this – his affair with Comfort, his fatherhood – because history had too strong a hold on him, because his bonds with Ezekiel had been too close. Perhaps just as he was on his way, he felt the tiny perfect wrists of his daughter pull on his legs. Perhaps he felt the clamp of her teeth as she bit into him, as she tried to make him help her scoop up all those fish. But dawn came and Isaiah awoke and he did not see her, he could not. He did not feel her, he could not. All he felt was empty; all he saw was that it had to end, he was not made to be a man, a father, an orphan, alone, and the only thing left was their ghosts. Isaiah walked towards the Lion Rock. His eyes blank-blank, his body rigid, his motions automatic.

*　　*　　*

Did the Lion Rock feel a pain tear through its heart that day – when the howls of anguish rose up to the clouds because a seven-year-old girl realised her father was gone? Did the seas part and the flax bow down and the fish, such as they were, swirl in circles trying to let the noise of her grief spread out and dissipate in that sad night air?

The gods watched as Isaiah arced out into the bay. The gods watched and did nothing.

Part Two

One

All three of them are childless. Nor have they married, it is far too late now and in the days when they might have, there were no girls – only fish. Dublin Small knows love only through his friendships. He is friends with the sea and the village, he is friends with the bay and since boyhood he has known the two Johnnies and yes indeed, down to the marrow of their very souls, they are friends.

For many of the fishermen, it had been too much: to stay in a village where they could not find a wife seemed unendurable and once the stocks of fish started to dwindle, the young men left – for the town perhaps, for another village that offered greater prospects. Dublin has stayed because he knows nowhere else. He has stayed because he is not a greedy man, because he has a deep core of idleness that runs through his bones, because he is content where he is, because he is afraid of what he might find outside. The two Johnnies have stayed because they do not see that their world is incomplete. They could not imagine that marriage or intimate relations of any kind could possibly improve their lot. Like Dublin, they too are content.

And now, thanks to the fish-storm, everything has changed. Friendships that Dublin thought he knew have been rearranged. The bay has surprised him, the sea has attacked him; Isaiah, whom Dublin has watched grow up, has disappeared and if Dublin looks out of the broken window of his hut where all four sit huddled in case the storm comes back, he can see that all the other families – the Cuckeltys and the Normans and Ivy Peacock and the rest – have packed up and left, have gathered up what little remained of their possessions so they could return to the town their forebears fled those eighty or so years before.

Dublin cannot remember what it was like to be a child. He looks at Athene Brown while she sits there huddled inside her blanket and he sees her petrified poor love, so wide-eyed sad, and he feels a hot cocktail of emotions course through him. Fear first, panic really – because she is so small; because what on earth are they to do with her, how on earth are they to look after her when for all these years they have struggled to look after themselves; fear again because what if she cries or hollers, what if she takes on all girly and woman-like, what if she shouts for her papa or cries for her papa and they look all over and they only find him dead? And Dublin feels pity too and shame because when she looks at him, it's so open, searching somehow; because he holds up his hand in front of his eyes and he sees hoary, sand-grained skin and how can that ever have been as soft, as elastic as hers; because she seems to see into him and what is he, what are they but three old men who do nothing, have done nothing; because what are men good for if they cannot care for their young. And then Dublin feels pity and fear and rage all at once, in a rush, because what in the world was the almighty thinking of when he made such a racket and a mess and left a little girl like her stranded.

The four sit in a square in Dublin's hut and it seems like hours. The two Johnnies fidget – they feel nervous, twitchy. The sky is slow to clear and what if it comes again, what if that vicious wind blows Dublin's hut over and they're all inside. The two Johnnies rub their temples, syncopating the rhythm of their fingers as though the one exists only to mirror the other. The Scotch they are drinking does not seem that good after all, a bit sour, but they keep sipping, sucking in their lips as they do so. No one smiles – they are all too afraid.

And it goes on like that for a few days, maybe a week. The old men are courteous and they bring her food and they bring her water and they let her sleep in the bed while they doze in the chairs. They sweep the floor a bit, they shift when she shifts and clear their throats when she does but it is not natural this isn't not at all. They are tripping over one another, they are jostling for space, three old men who are not just ancient and stiff and gruff but also inexperienced in love and now here she is, sitting there – in a rocker – or lying there – on the bed – or walking about in the sand with her feet dragging and her head hanging and they are all sad, they cannot help themselves, to see a child in this way, to see her alone when she's only so young.

Sometimes at night while she sleeps and they sit out on the sand, between grunts and occasional sips from their cups because there's still more of that filthy Scotch to get rid of, they talk about her: talk about her sad deep eyes and how's as she should be playing games or building sandcastles or telling stories or joined up with other children. They wonder about her mother – none of them knew Comfort – and fleetingly about Isaiah and Ezekiel before him. And the three of them are vexed for her – old hearts creaking with pity, old livers moaning in sympathy.

But one day Athene smiles at them – when they bring her some soup and it is hot, when the storm has long gone and the skies are clear and crisp, when the winds are chill and she is hungry and they are right there to meet her needs – and all of a sudden, the old men feel something new, something new indeed. Old age suddenly presents them with a compensation. She is a tiny dazzling jewel.

It turns into love.

Dublin might not know it, might not say it but it changes him, makes him younger, and for the first time in his life, he becomes busy. Ignores the screams from his joints and sets to, cleaning up the beach, throwing away the fish, burning the debris of boats, rearranging the carvings on the eaves of his hut because for years now, they have been in need of some work. Sometimes all three of them work at it, they are all huffing and groaning and creaking and they are all toiling away for her, doing their level best to make things better for her. They make piles across the beach of the things that have been scattered and there are heaps of coloured stones and some leaves of mica so Athene sits down among the piles and she remakes some chimes with leaves of mica and pieces of cuttlefish and she listens to them as they ring again with the sound of the sea.

Soon they come to agree that they are all too cramped in Dublin's place so they set to, old men heaving, old men pushing, to lift up the red hut – Samuel's – to right it and then she can have her home back, her tiny wooden bed back in its allotted corner and they can watch over her, let her have some space. So she comes to live not with them but next to them, not breathing their air but watched over by them from the veranda or the dunes behind or the flat beach in front.

And slowly she comes to smile a bit more – as time eases past and they become friends, as the shock of Isaiah's disappearance wanes – and even she plays games with them, tinkers with their pipes or runs off with their old shoes or mixes up their rods so's they have to rearrange them all because each one likes his set up differently. For her, they wake up spry and it is new, a feeling of expectation and sometimes they argue among themselves because this rush of love, it is intoxicating and each is as keen as the other to experience it more.

Dublin Small sits on watch at night and he wonders at his extraordinary good fortune. He thought he had known everything – and the gods have granted him something more.

*   *   *

And their love grows and blossoms. While Dublin Small feels young again, the two Johnnies are frisky and light-hearted. The bay – for all that it is empty now – fulfils a purpose and you would think that there crept onto the lips of the Lion the smallest hint of a smile.

With a child among them, the old men find their lives washed with a soft gentility. Dublin runs his hand over his scalp and it feels smooth, pure. The twins poke their fingers in their ears – there is always sand in there – and the white tufts of hair that peep from inside feel like thistledown. A routine descends – one they can vaguely recall from their own childhood – where food and sleep, washing and exercise mark the passing of time in strict but reassuring sections and Dublin finds himself raking through the sand to bring in clams or pushing out the last remaining boat to wait for fish, while the two Johnnies talk to her or walk with her or help her with the washing or play games with her in the shadow of the Lion.

And they teach her, all three of them, the lessons she had begun with her father – the lessons of the winds and the tides, the hymn of the rains and the prayers of the gulls who swarm inland when typhoons rage at sea. They teach her a kind of self-sufficiency – of the imagination, of mind and body – that years later, she is always grateful for: how to fill in the time, how to gentle the time, not eat it but nurse it lazily in the palm of your hand so that it does not hang too heavy; how to sit, just sit and watch and in some small way grow, from observing the tiny, perpetual movement of the sands or the never-ending circles of the birds or the way the flaxes blow or the constant drifts of the seaweed as they ebb and flow, up the beach, down the beach.

They teach her to eke out her survival – from the fish, such as there are, from the apple trees on the ridge and the other fruit trees, from the wasteland and the cutty-grass, and they troop up, over the dunes, with a sack or two, a basket, and pick whatever they can find – cherries, apples, crab-apples, maybe wild peaches or plums; elderberries too and these Dublin uses to make wine, sweet and sickly but aromatic and deep gold and they share it sometimes, all four, growing giggling-roaring-hiccup drunk, rolling on their backs like old ewes with their lamb and the gods smile because the sound of their laughter is too infectious to be ignored.

There are high days, there are low days. There are times when they can feast and more when they all go a little hungry so she can eat. They have songs that they sing – old tunes, old words that blur together, blend in with the winds. Sometimes there are stories, legends of the sea, tales of Samuel, his prowess as a sailor, his ferocity as a man. Sometimes there are games or dances but these do not last for long, the old men quickly grow tired.

And then there are walks – because often, there is nothing else so they just walk, at dusk or at dawn, it does not matter, smell of a hot land awakening or a hot land that is going to sleep and they troop along in a short, eager crocodile. Along the top of the ridge so they can see the ocean on one side; the fields and in the far distance the crooked chimneys of the town on the other. Walking and they might say nothing, they might not even share a tune but they hold one of her hands, sometimes both and they are enmeshed in their shadows, dancing in and out of the pebbles, unconscious of time.

Athene Brown is wrapped in a soft veil of childhood. She does not pause to ask questions, she is seven-eight-nine and the old men care for her as she requires. Tears for the loss of Isaiah have blown away on the sea and Athene lives in the moment. She is free. Wild barefoot free. Free to go and explore, even as far as the top of the Lion, even as far as the end of the bay and beyond, as far as the plain that fringes the ridge that looks out over the lace-edged waters of their ocean.

Free. Today she is running and dancing, tomorrow she will run and dance some more. Today she is leaning under the chin of the Lion with the sea at her feet, singing songs at the top of her voice, arching her neck and her back as she rolls with the echo and the lilt of her tune. Tomorrow she will go down this path, that path, down tracks with stones, tracks with no stones. She will look in bushes, she will peer at plants, she will count the insects, then lose count because there are so many, they come they go so busy, so quick.

Or she will visit the rocks at the south end of the bay – when the tide is out and the weather is good – and she will slither over the top, her toes curling into the damp moss, and she will watch the minnows or the cockles or the molluscs or the tiny sea anemones and soon Athene comes to know the rise of the tides and the way of the winds because she has waited for them, there on the rocks, watching the planet as it breathes, as the blood seeps in its veins, in, out, in, out, bringing men from here, birds from there, boats from here, men from there.

She watches the soft pools fill and the green-lipped mussels as they cling to the stone and she knows the weather as though it were her own and she sees the shrimp as they float past in clouds and always she watches the sky, waits for a change in case the sea will roar in and the pools blend into one.

And then she comes back from an hour from three from a day in the spread of the bay back to where it all belongs, back to the clackety steps and the door that does not open, does not close, to Dublin Small and the twins, to her old red shanty and their old green shanty beside. For here is the place she knows best, here where strands of her hair are caught in the woodwork, where the dots of her tears are cast as stains on the rough wood floor, here where she learns to dream and she learnt to breathe.

And maybe instead of running wild, Athene Brown will just sit and suck it all in – the way her bed never sits against the wall, the way it always runs into the middle because that is where it wants to be; the way the wind blows through and you can sit there and let it tickle the roots of your hair – or the rain, as it sweeps across the floor on those days in the wet season when there is nowhere else for it to go; or the light, as it jumps off the pieces of mirror and leaps onto the coloured shells, as it glints on the leaves of mica that blow, now and always, with the sound of the sea.

She can sit on the clackety steps – years beyond, years before – close her eyes and there it would be, the beach, the rattling of the reeds, the memory of her father's footsteps as he walked back thuck-thuck through the sand from another day in his boat; the float of her mother's ghost, the rattly rumble of the old men as they grunt their way into more frugal days.

Or she can sit at Dublin's feet while he tells some of the tales that hide under his cap – tales of the fish in the sea and the fish that have all now gone; the tale of Samuel, all over again – the places where he walked, the paths that he carved out of the hill, the plants that he tended, the intricate carvings that he pierced in the driftwood canopy of his hut. Stories of the man's ferocious face. Stories of his rage and his strength and his gruffness and the curses he could bring down upon the townspeople if he felt so inclined. And more than that, stories of Samuel's skill at sea, of those extraordinary powers which should surely be reserved only for gods and angels. Fish would leap up to him, chase him, throw themselves into his wake. Green-lipped mussels would fall at his feet in fistfuls, shrimp would chase him through the soft velvet pools that lay between the claws of the Lion's feet.

Here in the precious nuggets of lazy afternoons she can reach out and touch it, she can rub her hands along it or lean her head against it, she can hear it, she can breathe it – here in the bay where her memories are carved and she can stay up, all day, well into the night, singing as she goes – through the caves, through the trees, over the ridge above – sing, sing, while her shadow crawls and creeps over the sands, silhouetted against the burning orange tapestry of an evening sky.

Two

Each night the old men, Dublin especially, go to sleep with renewed vigour. Athene Brown has brought them joy, she has brought them hope and they look forward to sleep so they can wake again, so they can plan more days with her, so they can argue gently between them over which of the three can spend more time with their precious charge.

But the seasons rise and fall with the tides and Athene Brown grows away from her magical seven-year-old innocence and a small cloud begins to form. Dublin Small may be old, he may be new to this kind of love, he may be idle and soft as a sea-sponge – but Dublin is no fool. He sees this cloud, clear as day. It is full of questions. It hovers over Athene Brown as she moves from being a girl to becoming a woman. It is full of girl-questions and woman-questions (about which, for sure, not one of the old men knows a whit). It is full of what-will-we-do-next questions and what-will-she-do-when-we-die questions and at last, when Dublin Small is leaving his eightieth year, he comes to know not just the joy of love but the pain of love. It has come but it must go. She is a child and now she is nine-ten-eleven, soon she will be twelve-thirteen-fourteen. She will be alone when they die, she will be ill-equipped, she will have to leave and how on earth will she do that when all they have done together is learn to survive here, in Samuel's Bay?

And the cloud bears another question, a big dirty one which none of them dares to ask because each is jealous of this love and anxious to preserve it – and that is, what on earth happened to him, where on earth did Isaiah go? Dublin Small has kept it to himself but he knows that the other two noticed it also: there were no signs of him. There was no hint that he had died or been battered on the rocks, there were no planks from his boat or splinters, there were no shreds from his shirt – and if he died in the storm, Dublin is pretty damned sure they would have known, they would have found something, the Deadmen would have thrown up a clue, no matter how small.

And above all the questions – as they sit around the fire toasting a fish or they walk along the ridge, slowly because they are still old, or they play boules in the shadow of the Rock with the breeze whirring on the jack, stealing their best shots – this question looms the largest and it frightens them because what if she notices and what if she asks them to tell her the truth.

And then one day, when she is twelve or so, when her thirst for knowledge pushes beyond the names of the flowers and the way of the winds, Athene Brown does ask them. She says what happened to Isaiah. She says what happened to my father and it is evening, there has been a high tide today, there are pieces of seaweed strung around the props of their hut and it is cold now, they have lit a bonfire, and dark and the old men shudder, hiding in the shadows beneath their caps.

No one knows how to answer her. No one knows how to lie, to say we do not know what happened to him or we think Isaiah died in the storm. They are old men, kind men, honest in their way and it would be wrong to deceive her, she looks at them and she has bold eyes and somehow they know she will know that they lie. Dublin Small lights a cheroot. He lets the smoke curl into the smoke from the fire. He clears his throat as he always does when he lights up but he feels sure she must be able to hear the note of discomfort that rings in his cough. Dublin Small answers her. He says it in such a low voice that Athene Brown has to ask him again, she has to say what did you say. She has to say it a third time too because Dublin is so afraid of the effect of his words and then even when he is pretty sure she has heard him she repeats the question what did you say – and Dublin knows she has taken it as badly as they had always feared she might.

The next day, they lose her. Dublin looks for her in the barley-sugar cave and all the inlets and he clambers up into the clearing in the cutty-grass so he can scan the bay. He looks in the red hut, in his own, he looks under the chin of the Lion and Dublin quivers because he had never expected this, to feel so distraught about someone at this stage in his life.

And there is no sign of her. Dublin comes back to his hut and the two Johnnies catch his eye but they all know there is

71

no point in asking have you found her because it is evident from the hang of their heavy heads that they have not.

They lose her for a day and then another. She has disappeared and the old men, who never weep, are almost ready to do so because how will she survive out there and what if she does not come back and what if she has been swept out to sea . . .

They scan the beach, the rocks, the ridge above, they scan all their haunts. They shout out – old men's voices wrapping themselves in the whip of the wind – and there is no reply, no echo. Then in the early dawn of the third day, Dublin Small finds her at last when he notices a trail of footsteps in the wet sand of an ebbing tide and he follows it and there she is, in a hole carved out between the floor of her hut and the beach – not crying or singing, not laughing but sitting there, shrunk down into the cowl of her shoulders, blank-eyed. He teases her out, lying on his stomach with ants marching over the back of his neck. His hips prod needles into him and when he has hugged her as she crawls towards him beneath the props of the hut, he has to ask her to give him a hand because it is not so easy for an old man to lie down like that.

So the young girl comes out and she pulls him up and he hugs her hard and they say nothing but both of them know that it will never be the same after this.

They watch as Athene begins to move away from them. She has her own troubles and she wanders in and out of the empty huts, picks up old jugs and the odd plate, turns them over, lets the weight of them sit in her hand and then she takes them back to her red hut when they cannot see her, hoarding things, piling up defences. She begins to swap things and Dublin might come in one evening and find the chairs, the table, the bed have all been exchanged for different models, ones she has dragged back through the dunes all alone, just a twelve-year-old girl.

They see her in new clothes too, ones that the women with their washing bottoms did not take or had lost and soon Athene is changing all her landscapes, becoming a man or a boy, a fisherman or a gipsy woman or a sailor. They see her in a wardrobe of disguises and there are hats and there are sticks and there are old shoes that drift in on the tide and she seems to lose herself, walking the boundaries of places the old men cannot guess at because all they have explored are the pages of an old encyclopaedia.

They see her grow taller and thinner. They see her face that was round and burnished by the sun and now it is longer and of course there is laughter, from time to time, but it is tinged with melancholy and sometimes it fades into the sea-wind too soon, too quick.

Through the thin cloud of smoke from his cheroot, Dublin watches the pain that came over her that evening by the bonfire as it bruises her; as she grows from twelve to thirteen to fourteen to fifteen and it runs round the corridors of her conscience, showing her all the possibilities she no longer has, all the hope that has been taken away. Sometimes she eats, sometimes she does not but gets up from the sandy floor, wanders off, drapes herself in clothes that do not fit, trying out new faces, new voices. She looks out to sea – they

73

watch her, when she has climbed the Lion Rock. They make out her profile while she sits with her chin in her hands in the clearing in the cutty-grass. Sometimes they hear her – words in a rumble, only they cannot make out what it is she says.

And Dublin's head fills with expletives, raging furious bloody hells because he cannot help her. Because he cannot protect her. Because he cannot shove it away, because he cannot hold up a hand and stop the push of time, because she is not his and he never had his own and she belongs to no one, not any more. Dublin wants to leap up out of his chair and become Isaiah. He wants to watch her smile spill out over her chin and lift up her steps as it did when she was younger. He wants to leap up out of his chair and wrap her in his craggy hug and take her back to the days when they just walked together, when they were old men and she was a child and it was soft gentility and nothing more.

Athene Brown is sixteen and Dublin Small is eighty-seven. The two Johnnies are in their late seventies. They have had nine years together in the bay – nine years and she has brought them more happiness than any of them could have anticipated. She has taught them many things – she, a girl! – not only love but practical things, how to read, even, in the case of the two Johnnies, how to write. Her appetite for knowledge, her energy has brought them all to huddle round some old encyclopaedia which was left by the storm and with Dublin's help they have unlocked its secrets, they have journeyed outside the bay and tasted something of the strange worlds beyond. She has made them things – a set of cards – from mother-of-pearl and slivers of razorfish, inset with pebbles – and played poker with them also, in the dark of their huts or under the only tree that gives any shade from the sun. Sometimes she has smoked with them, rolled cheroots with Dublin Small and watched their smoke as it entwined in the wind; and she has made them laugh because she is alive, this girl, full of a vigour they are too old to remember, and they have sat there – of an evening when the sun is bleeding into the sea and the winds have at last relented – in a circle and they have passed round the jug of Scotch and the cheroots, taken a puff, a swig, then sat in the swirl of the smoke and let the haze come down slowly, as though it were not there already.

But the wind of change that first blew up when she found out, it brings with it something else, something that Dublin has tried to ignore but no longer can. Dublin is dying. Dublin's chest is filling up with old pus, he can feel it every day. The village is empty but for them and where for a while it had a sense of purpose, now it smells of decay and Dublin wakes up each morning feeling more and more besieged by this wretched rotten smell of old men and the past and unwanted change.

Dublin takes a swig of elderberry wine. It is sweet and rich but to him, today, it tastes of dirty water. Dublin takes a puff on his cheroot but it makes him cough, a cough so long and deep that for a moment, Dublin has a glimpse of oblivion. Dublin sits back on his chair, scuffs the sand with his feet, draws a picture of a fish, looks out over the sea, laughs at the irony of it because for years he was ready to die and now, when it is time, he finds himself damn well flaming well needed.

For one last time his memory rolls out before him – minke whales and a sea teeming with fish, albatrosses soaring on the currents above a mauve-and-lace-fringed ocean, Samuel's boat glinting on the Deadmen and the fires on the top of the Lion for the fishermen who had died and the women and the children and the Carnival of the Fish and young men wrestling with marlin until you thought they would never be able to carry on. For one last time, he sees Athene Brown on the floor of his hut with her legs crossed and a drift of hair hanging by her cheek. Chinks of sunlight catching on her face and she is not talking, only somewhere else, wintergreen eyes shining maybe with tears, maybe excitement, who knows where she is; and, of all the pictures, Dublin Small chooses this one for she is he thinks at that moment more beautiful than anything he has ever seen, more beautiful than the sight of the minke mother and her calf basking on the rocks in the sun, more beautiful than the necklaces of all those fish or the sight of the pyres licking up to the clouds from the peak of the Lion Rock.

Dublin mutters through his rasping breath bloody buggering typical. And then time passes and Dublin no longer knows what is happening and he never will again.

And they are too old to help her, they are too stiff, they are too overwrought with grief and shock even to look at Dublin's dead eyes so she has to do it alone, she has to carry Dublin Small up to the top of the Lion Rock alone. They tell her and she does not cry. She comes back from the barley-sugar cave where she had been lying down, counting the stripes in the ceiling, and she sees him there and she sees the twins dancing about in despair and she picks him up.

He is not too heavy because inside his old shirts and his old trousers, he had shrunk to the size of a boy. The two Johnnies watch as she walks towards the Lion Rock. Sweat must ooze from her forehead. Small screams must seep from her muscles because she is young and not yet so strong. She scales the rock – over the waves because that is the only side you can readily climb – and the two Johnnies try to will her up and forwards, not wishing to contemplate what would happen if she fell. She grabs for tufts of grass and she grips the sticky-out stones and, their broken hearts in their mouths, they watch as she eases him – intact – onto the top of Lion Rock where all their friends, their forebears, the villagers they have known since childhood have been cremated.

And they wait – sitting in their chairs in the sand, limp with grief, silent with grief – until the Rock is swallowed by the sea-dark sky and she lights a fire, adding fish-oil and seaweed to the flames so that the waters glow for miles around with tiny falling sparks of their old dead friend.

And the wind of change does not ease up, it blows harder. Now it ruffles the tufts of hair in the ears of the two Johnnies, whispering to them, beckoning them. Athene Brown can feel it, she talks to them, hugs their legs, helps them now where before they helped her. She runs errands for them. She boils water for their cups and for their morning toilet. She holds up the mirror so they can see to scratch their chins and she cooks things, trying to tend the vegetables, pick the berries, bottle the fruits, rake in a few fish, all that without letting them see just how hard it is without the old bugger there to cheer them on.

But at night the sky between their huts is racked with sobs and it becomes clear, after just a few days, that life can no longer go on as it was. In one cruel stroke, it becomes clear how they depended on Dublin not just for his crusty old bloody old mindedness, but for his sense – because it was he who caught any fish they could eat and he who showed them how to mend the huts when they were damaged by the wind. The twins become wheedling and whiny. They forget about the good times they have enjoyed with Athene Brown among them and they forget the lesson that love has taught them and they moan all day, sometimes getting up, walking around, sometimes just sitting there, staring. The years that they shed when she was younger are all assumed once more. Two old men, not mourning their friend, only helpless, devoid of hope and you might be afraid for them, you might be afraid too for Athene Brown because they do not seem too good, sitting there like that – but then the wind whispers to them that they could follow Ivy Peacock, they could go to the town.

And the idea breaks through the layers of sand and it lodges in their minds. The two Johnnies say nothing, they do not mention it to Athene Brown. For a few years prised apart by their love for her and their mission to take care of her, now they merge again into one and they forget her and they set their single-minded sights on the row of crooked chimneys that you can make out from the top of the ridge if you look hard.

*　　*　　*

Athene Brown wakes up one morning and it is seven days and eight nights since Dublin Small died. There is a hot wind and it fills the air so you cannot hear your thoughts, only banging. Athene rolls out of her tiny bed, too small for her now. She wraps a sequin cloth around her hair, she puts a cowrie-shell bracelet on her wrist, she remembers with a stab that Dublin is gone.

And she moves slowly. There is no sound from the twins, only the noise of the banging but that must be the wind and Athene feels too tired, too sad to hurry.

Perhaps, if she had dressed more quickly, she might have seen which way they had gone. She might have been able to shout stop wait for me, she might not have found herself alone in Samuel's Bay. But Athene comes out of her red hut and she sees the door of an empty Dublin's hut flapping and that is all.

Three

The cool river that plies the town runs along the side of the main street like a deep dark ribbon. Isaiah never tires of the view. He sits here on a creel and watches the gulls as they swoop behind the boats, watches the men as they shout and the dogs on the prows and the children. If he can, Isaiah comes here at dawn. He does not speak for here there is no need for words but he listens to the honky-tonk of an unfurling day and he feels grand.

How many years is it since Isaiah ran away, since the fish-storm changed everything, since Isaiah saw that the gods were cruel and he was unable to withstand their attack? Ask Isaiah and he could not remember. Look in his eyes and you will see they are hooded, cloudy, many of their secrets long mislaid. How many years has he spent in this town – with its crooked chimneys and its big hopes and its windows and all those wooden huts lined up cheek by jowl – and Isaiah could only guess because to him, Samuel's Bay is a faint memory.

Now there are lines on his face. There is grey in his hair, there are flaps of drooping skin across his belly and the muscles that he used with such joy – when he bent down to pick her up, when he leant out of the boat to pull her towards him – are flaccid, edging towards redundancy.

Isaiah cannot tell you how long he has been here but for sure, he has thought many times of his daughter. Sometimes he sees her face. Her wintergreen eyes, her dark jutting cheekbones. The air she had that was so like Comfort's, wispy and watchful, and yet there was something else about her – even so young as seven – that made her utterly herself. Maybe the way her chin stuck out when she felt challenged. Maybe the way she crossed her arms and stood with her tummy out front and her bottom out back and it gave her a force, as though you would hesitate to doubt her.

There are times when Isaiah hears a voice and he stops, looks around, it could almost be hers. Times when Isaiah closes his eyes, perhaps he is tired, when he lets himself drift towards sleep and there they are, tiny fingers shaking his arm, making him wake up, there are things to do, places to explore. Once Isaiah awakens and he feels a pain, sharp pain, in his calf and he looks down, there is a moon-shaped pattern of teeth-marks embedded in his leg.

Or perhaps Isaiah is not ambushed by memory but he seeks it out, he thinks back to specific days. He relives that day when they all played boules, Athene, Isaiah, Dublin, the two Johnnies, one or two others. There was a keg of Scotch, there was a bottle or two of elderberry wine. It was one of many hot days in a long dry season and there was no wind but there was laughter and there was an epic match, it seemed Isaiah could do no wrong this day, and he looked round once or twice, he saw her watching him, saw her sharp eyes willing him on to win.

From his rescue by the bargemaster, Isaiah came to slowly – on the side of the river, on the outskirts of a town where no one knew him; in surroundings he did not know, in air that did not taste at all the same. There were warehouses – small, low-slung factories with steamy, smoky atmospheres. There were shops – wooden cabins with small faces peeping out do you want something sweet sir, do you want something fresh? Spices – rich, dark, exotic, orange, hot and the air laden with dust and the promise of food and sometimes you could hear coins clinking and the small faces would break into smiles. There was music – stringy, twangy, nasal – and there were dogs with no hair and dogs with hair. There were rats trailing in and out of the cabins and sometimes a beggar and there was no sign of the relentless wind or the blowing sand and at first Isaiah twirled round on his axis, stunned by all this because it was so far from anything he had really known.

He went to the shops. He went to the warehouses, the market, the bazaar. In the wake of his brush with death, Isaiah wandered automatic through the new experience of the town – unable to judge or to stop or to know who he was, unable to say I am a fisherman, I do not belong here. He soaked it all in – the hustle and the crush and the pell-mell of city living and he bounced from one body to the next, one line of people to the next and he was only a shadow.

Why did Isaiah not chase his own death with more vigour? Why did he not drop the coloured stones he had placed in his pockets and follow them, down to the seabed where it was dark and all worry would be extinguished? It was a question that in those early days and weeks Isaiah posed to himself a thousand times – as he found himself in the outskirts of the town and he brought curses on the barge-children who had saved him; as he coughed and coughed his way through those early nights because there was still some salt water within him; as his lungs slowly recovered sufficiently and he was able to get up, move around, look for food.

Did he believe she had died? Did he think in his heart of hearts that the storm had taken her and that was why he left? Did he reassure himself – night after night, as he sat out in the dust-dirt streets, as he waited for an answer, as he hoped that someone or something might come and save him from the prospect of some meandering, half-lit life – that there was no point in returning to Samuel's Bay, that she was gone, that she and all the rest had surely been killed by the storm and all he had left now was to wait for another opportunity to lie down and die himself?

Maybe the town sowed a seed in him. Maybe the strangeness of the town did not repel Isaiah as it might have, but drew him. Maybe the sudden release of all those pressures, the lure of something new and different, the fluke of being saved, they all added up and Isaiah, who believed he was leaving Samuel's Bay as he was leaving this planet – for ever – could not help himself. He clung to life.

Because he must eat, he took work. He did anything, anything and they gave him a bit here, a bit there. Sometimes it was a day's labour, sometimes it was an hour or two. He carried boxes and sorted fruit, he gutted chickens, even – when he must – he gutted fish. He swept floors, he cleaned filthy kitchens, he washed bricks, he scrubbed floors. He did not understand hierarchy or rules or politics or yappy voices but he worked as instructed, kept his head snapped in tight to his neck.

He walked further – to the furthest factories, to the villas on the hill, to the outermost cabin shops where he used to bring bits of booty to sell all those years before. He said I can work I can help can you pay me and he was not afraid, he went in, stood there, mumbled out these words and sometimes they said yes and sometimes they did not even look up to hear who was speaking.

And after work, Isaiah walked the town. Sucked in its life, learnt its contours beneath the thip-thap of his fisherman's sandals. He learnt its tides as he had learnt those of the sea. He watched the people, he watched the cats, he watched the weeds that clung to the sides of walls while vehicles scurried by, he watched pieces of paper blowing in sudden circles. Even sounds he traced, the trail of a bang or a scritch or a clunk as it made its way through the dust-laden air and Isaiah was proud to think he had understood it, he had traced its source. Every patch of grass, every street, every dry ditch, every lump in the road came to know Isaiah's tread; every corner, every stray dog, every drain.

And above all the river. All rivers lead to the sea and Isaiah sat on a creel, his eyes running right to left as he followed the drift of its cargo. Sometimes he would return the wave of a child, hum in his head the exact note of a hooter. He would lose himself in the passage of a sea-bird, in the conversations of gulls or the progress of a bow-wave as it grew and died and here, he found calm.

At last, after how many years in the city he cannot recall, Isaiah is granted a place in a warehouse. This time, it is not for a day or an hour but Isaiah becomes one of a row of men and women, heads down, hands out. They weave silk here. Tiny strands of fabric dance in the air. Bottles of brilliant dye sit in corners. Looms dance, shuttles dance and Isaiah works hard, sweat seeping down from his temples. At the end of his shift, he runs his hand along the cloth, watches the sheen as it catches on the sunlight – when the burrs on his fingers snag the slub, Isaiah puts it down, walks away.

He finds a small cabin on the mudflat at the outskirts of the town and he paints it red and he adorns the gables with wooden carvings. He finds a chair – someone has dropped an old chair off the bridge; and a wind-up gramophone which he winds up, listens to Kitty someone as she warbles out arias from operas whose names he does not understand. He has money for tobacco, money for a fish sometimes and these he eats with a tight smile because he knows how much it must have cost someone to bring it to his table.

He walks the town. Some days he looks up and sees a child, receives an unconditional smile. Some days the sun shines on him, from above, unstopped by the shadows of the tapestry of buildings. Maybe light catches on the stained-glass window of the church and flashes multi-coloured pictures over the road; or the evening reflection of a warehouse is captured until it dances on the still of the river; maybe the sounds of all those people, the screech from all those wheels blend into chords and if he closes his eyes he can almost hear that it is music; or maybe Isaiah becomes embroiled sometimes in a crowd – women from the warehouses, people going here and there, an audience for a street-show – and Isaiah is among them, he is one of them, he heaves when they heave, shouts, laughs, jeers when they do and he is as connected as each of them, alone and together, man among many.

And then Isaiah comes across an old acquaintance – just like that. One day, he is walking the streets alone and the next, he is walking, side by side, with a man he has known since he was a child.

It happens during the gathering. The gathering is when they all come – all the farmers around – to bring in and sell their wool. Isaiah has watched this once or twice and it has taken him back to the days when he was at Samuel's Bay, to the Carnival of the Fish. When all the people scrub up their faces; when cheeks shine and boots shine and there are smiles and expectation rings throughout the air because TodayisaParty. When all the gossip is exchanged and all the tut-tuts, when deaths and marriages, births and tragic collapses are ooed and aaed over; when flagons of beer are drunk; when the morning wakes up bright and is filled with business; when the afternoon turns a little hazy and the evening in its turn roars – with pleasure and indulgence – and then the next morning, there is only pain, only heavy heads and whydidwedoits and neveragains.

Isaiah flanks the crowd of wool-sellers and wool-buyers.

He watches the mill-owners as they size up the fleeces. He watches the farmers and the dealers, the ones who are watchful and the ones who in their turn are subject to relentless scrutiny. There is a huge fluffy mountain in the market square and there are children and women with their best dresses on and there are shouts and cries and why-helloos and no sign of striking workers, no sign of the hairless dogs. Isaiah does not take the glass of beer that is offered to him from a table but he walks round the body of humanity, listens to the hum. Rain threatens but it seems to pass over, chased away no doubt by the determined wall of gaiety that greets it down below.

Isaiah marvels at the wool. He listens to the tic-tac of the dealers, the tic-tac clink-plink as the coins fall into their pockets. He watches the dry smiles of those who have dealt well and the tight lips of those who have been cheated. He remembers the Carnival of the Fish, the glinting muscles of the young men wrestling with the marlin; the young men then wrestling with one another when there were no longer any fish left to fight. With a gasp of nostalgia, Isaiah goes to sit down because goodness me, he is beginning to feel his age – and he turns round, to say excuse me to someone whom he has bumped into, to ease his passage through the wall of bodies so that he can run from this, hide from this – and he finds himself staring at Frank Armstrong.

Frank Armstrong who was always handy with a tool. Frank Armstrong who must have left at the same time as he did, who says he's been here fifteen, twenty years now, whose life as a craftsman has its ups and downs. Isaiah is taken aback to see a familiar face. The flush of nostalgia grips at his stomach and the older man places a hand on the younger man's back to be sure there is nothing too badly wrong.

They take to meeting. For some reason, neither alludes to Samuel's Bay but they sit there, together – at times on the barrels by the river, at others on the steps to the church or on the road that leads up to the grand villas on the hill. Frank Armstrong has a family now. He has children – he married late in life – and he works in a mill, mending things. It's not what I imagined, he says to Isaiah. I miss the sea, he says. But that is as close as they come to talking about old times.

Instead, they make new times. Frank Armstrong likes to gamble. The town has shown him a new pleasure – in place of elderberry wine and boules on the sand – and Frank takes Isaiah to a back-street hovel where men sit in circles, no words. The air is filled with smoke. No one looks up from their game. No one seems to speak and it takes Isaiah a while to gather just exactly what they are doing, what is being lost and what won. He goes to ask Frank but Frank has left him, he is sucked into a circle somewhere else, grunting a bit, digging out the tic-tac coins from his pocket, handing them over.

They meet every week – sometimes at the end of a market-day, sometimes a day or so later. They find a routine – Frank comes and finds Isaiah on his creel, watching the river on its unstoppable journey to the sea. Isaiah stands up. The two men shake hands. They walk to the den.

Isaiah starts his gambling with only a coin or two, with a penny or a match. He takes a while to learn the language, to learn the signals spoken by hands and fingers, cards and sliding money. His addiction is slow to kindle, yet he is quick to find solace in the place and years later he asks himself why. This is as far from life on the sea as you could picture – far from the hot winds and the Lion Rock and the day-in-day-out struggle for existence. Here men are immobile, corpulent, eyes lit with pleasure. Here men talk only to themselves and it is not the same as chasing the shade on the sand playing boules, not the same as sitting with Ezekiel in front of a smoky bark-fire. Here time goes as fast as you wish it to go.

Perhaps it is another persona he can hide behind – a night-time Isaiah. An Isaiah pushing further away the failure of his time in Samuel's Bay; pushing further away the elements of nature that he fought so fruitlessly. An Isaiah so embraced by the city, by the ways of city man, that he can turn to himself in all apparent honesty and say I have changed, I was never destined for that life. And perhaps too there is an element of self-knowledge, an element of guilt that chases him towards the gamblers. He can sit here among men who do not talk, who keep their secret wrapped tight within and it is all right, he is not betraying the memory of those he has loved, only he is still alone.

Sometimes in the years that follow Isaiah dangles the possibility of suicide once more in front of his aching eyes. He contemplates trying to drown again – perhaps in the river this time. He thinks of throwing himself into one of the machines at the warehouse or setting light to himself with Scotch and tar and whatever else flammable he can find. Isaiah swings the prospect of another attempt at death back and forth.

And it does not come. He does not feel the need as he did then to drown or die or leave or just go, he does not feel the ache that surged then from his heart through his every muscle. Then there was fear, there was disappointment, there was shame. Then there was the grief for Comfort, for his father – grief that he had never aired. There was the joke of the gods who showered him in fish and there was something else, a young-man need to act, to sort things out, if necessary to die, perhaps to have some last thrill in life through death. Isaiah no longer feels the anguish of boredom and the agony of being overstretched, the days that drag behind and those that yawn in front and the chasm inside him, because he must do things and they must be right; he no longer feels the panic of energy and the drive and yet the boredom of energy because it will not let him rest.

Now Isaiah can sit on the creel, gentle the time in the circle of his vision. He can sit in the evenings with the cards and his stake waiting to be lost and believe there is no guilt. He has put aside all his demons. They chased him here and now Isaiah has found a life that embraces his solitude, a life arranged into neat, disposable packets and he can put one down, pick up another. He can put down the bay, pick up the town. He can pick up the night, put down the day and he might not exist, there might not be anyone to mark his passing, to note his arrival; there might be no one to dissipate the noise of his thoughts, to hear him, respond to him; but Isaiah sleeps now the sleep of the blameless.

And slowly he feels it. Slowly Isaiah lets Athene Brown recede into the mists of his past. He makes a picture of how it was and he sees her – every day – how she was sucked up by the storm. He sees her perfect child face – taken. He sees her home demolished, the bay abandoned, everyone killed or banished by the storm and he comes to believe that the gods were kind, to take her when she was so young, so perfect; to take her, to send him away, to save the fish from the fishermen by chasing the village into the town.

Isaiah acquires an unswerving belief in this version of events. His daughter died in the storm. She has joined the ghost of Comfort, the old bones of Ezekiel and she tiptoes through his dreams; and with this, Isaiah can let her go so that she fades into the warm hue of memory.

Four

B ut the unease that swept through Samuel's Bay those years before has slowly closed in from all sides on the town. This tiny island is being squeezed – sucked out from within by all the needs of all the people who will not open their eyes and see. There has been terrible weather – storms not just at sea but throughout the land. Crops have been lost, stock has been lost. Houses have blown down, rivers have spilt over and it seems, if you look at the pattern, that the fish-storm was just the beginning.

Isaiah's silk factory is in the centre of the town. How many people work there, Isaiah cannot tell but it is one of the largest and soon it becomes central to the malaise that blows in from the empty waters. The workers are beginning to cough. Of course they have always coughed, there have always been fibres floating on the air – but now there are showers of dust falling down from the roof. Perhaps it is all this weather, perhaps it is the wind that has rattled the timbers, who knows, but something must be done, something must be done.

A young man appears – to lead the workers through their

moment of strife; to uphold their struggle against the silk factory owners. The young man is eloquent, upstanding, unafraid and the workers cheer when he stands at the end of the line at the end of a hot day to talk fighting-talk. Isaiah pays no attention to all of this. When the end-of-day gong sounds, he walks back to the mudflat. He does not understand crowds and their anger, feels no part of this fight and he pulls his old fedora down around his ears, winds up Kitty someone, listens to her arias, waits for the restlessness to pass.

Yet it spreads, like a wild fire. Soon all the cabin shops and the little warehouses with their tiny struggling industries are hostage to people waving their arms, demanding an improvement in their fortunes. The young man who has come to the silk factory springs up as the young man to lead them all because, above all else, he has words. This is not a big town – there is a river to one side and a mudflat to the other. There are dust-dirt streets and patches of grass but the town, to Athene's island, is the main city, capital city – where the men with big ideas congregate; where the men with few prospects cling on like pieces of wet weed to slimy, sea-battered rock.

Isaiah hears the rumble of discontent as it ripples out through his town. His red cabin trembles. The mudflat shudders. One or two of the coloured stones he had placed in his pocket before he jumped from the Lion Rock fall off the ledges. Isaiah does not heed the signals but walks down to the side of the river where the old men sit and chew on sticks and count the barges and watch the currents swirling round the bridge. Isaiah sucks in his breath, sits down on his creel, inhales familiar smells.

They plan a strike. They hiss at the warehouse owner – when at last he comes to see them – and one of them throws an egg at him and the young-man-their-leader, flushed with indignation, goes up and demands a meeting and Isaiah is disgusted, the cheek of it. Isaiah begins to panic because he does not know what to do. He wishes to work but there are rows of angry men and women, standing at the gate to the warehouse, and Isaiah is afraid to cross the line, is afraid to cause trouble. He wishes to hide in the cool of his blood-red hut but he cannot buy food if he does not work. He wishes to run his finger along the slub of the fabric, to immerse himself in the routine he has now found, to look up when the line of the workers is hard at their task and see the heads down, watch the motes of dust and fibre as they dangle in the hot-sweat air.

Rains come and the workers who were coughing from the dust start coughing from the cold. Isaiah has to fight weather that he used to know by the sea but he has never seen here in the town. His mudflat transforms into a broad black bog and his cabin threatens to float away because the waters rise and rise. Isaiah, who talks to no one, becomes afraid again because the threat of the strike that might have receded now looms larger and the young man seems unstoppable in his crusade.

He no longer sleeps the sleep of the blameless but Isaiah finds his nights haunted by old visions. His birdoflove beckons him as she lies in the wind, ribbons blowing.

Ezekiel beckons him, from the other side of the Deadmen. A seven-year-old girl-child whispers something to him, words he cannot decipher, and Isaiah wakes, tormented by meaning he cannot grasp. Isaiah winds up his gramophone but Kitty someone only warbles sharp as she has always done. He tosses and turns in his bed, hoping to hide again in sleep, but there is no escaping it, Isaiah feels unnerved.

Isaiah dwells on his anxiety but that does nothing to disperse it. He tries to fill his heart with optimism. He walks up and down the dust-dirt streets and you see him, he is talking to himself, words you cannot unravel, wintergreen eyes scrunched up with tension.

His days are empty. There was the comfort of routine but someone has taken it from him. There was the nest of his cabin hut but someone has made it damp, stranded it in a foul-smelling swamp. There was sleep but that has changed and there are old memories waiting and Isaiah does not want to let them in.

At last Isaiah decides he will go and see the young man. He does not have a plan but he goes to the warehouse. The gates are shut and one or two women shoo him away and he asks them, he says where is the young-man-your-leader. Next Isaiah goes to a cabin in a back alley and it is tiny this cabin, smaller than Isaiah's own and there is a whole family in there, small faces merging like flowers in a bunch. Isaiah has come here, stomping. His steps have pressed into the dirt, pressed because Isaiah is troubled. Perhaps anger would be too strong for Isaiah but there is indignation, a kind of helplessness that has translated itself into something big for Isaiah. He marches up to the cabin and he bangs on the swinging door. He is going to say something. He is going to achieve something.

The young man is tall but slight. He smiles a big smile and he must be the oldest in the family but there are so many, it is hard to say. Isaiah says I need to work. He her-herms shyly and the words sound loud in his ears. They sit on barrels outside the cabin and the dust falls in layers on the young man's hair. The young man replies we all need to work. Isaiah says but you do not understand. The young man replies and neither do you.

An hour turns into a day and they sit, old man, young man, while the words rise up in steam around their heads. Mostly they are not Isaiah's words – the young man is filled with his mission. Isaiah is bombarded by the pride of the righteous, by the garrulousness of the proud. Isaiah hears the young man talk of the workers and they are his friends. He hears him talk of the scandal of the warehouse and the owners are not his friends. There is talk of the elements and all this weather as though it were part of the conspiracy and Isaiah does not respond, only he sits there. The young man says he will change it all. He will change the poorpay and the dustfromtheroof. He will change the coughingcoughingcoughing and you will see, what is your name again, you will see, things will be better after all.

Isaiah's present seems to be slipping through his fingers. He thought he had carved a life for himself where he could don each disguise and they suited him, he went unnoticed. At times he was a silk-worker, then a creel-sitter; at others a gambler and even now, reluctantly, an observer-of-militants.

But the gods seem to be pursuing him again – or maybe it is just that his disguises are not good enough – because now Isaiah finds some of his roles are being taken away. No more working in the warehouse; no more gambling, there are few who can afford the pleasure. Little creel-sitting, the unease means the old men are afraid to leave their houses.

And just as his present seems to be evanescing, so his past seems slowly to be making its reappearance. First there was Frank Armstrong. Now there is Ivy Peacock. Isaiah sees her in the distance at a meeting, she must work in one of the other warehouses, and he feels a shock run electric through his body. Ivy Peacock waves. She raises one eyebrow as though presented with a rich nugget of gossip and Isaiah shrinks inside because what on earth does that mean.

A few days later Isaiah comes across the Cuckeltys. Ron and his family, they are coming out of the church, they are not well dressed, Isaiah wants to run and hide but it is too late, is that you Isaiah! Isaiah listens while they say all the words you say to someone you have not seen for twenty years. He listens while they tell with rueful faces the tale of their time here; he winces while they relive the storm, while they dig up reminiscences he rather hoped he had lost. Why does Isaiah fear these old friends so? Ask him and he cannot say – after all, he believes he has no cause for guilt.

Then Frank Armstrong – who rarely speaks – happens to mention that the two Johnnies have died. He says will you

98

come to see them buried and Isaiah does not know whether to accept or refuse, he had no idea they were here, let alone still alive. But he knew they were once friends of his father and maybe it is that; or maybe it is just that, in spite of himself, he feels curious for in any case, Isaiah goes to the funeral.

He stands at the back, walks behind the cart with the coffins. He helps them push it – when it gets stuck in a rut because it's only him and Ivy and the Cuckeltys there to wave them off – and he helps them lower the boxes into the ground and inside he says words to them that come close to acknowledging the past but after, when it is just all the old people from Samuel's Bay, townspeople now, Isaiah does not wait, but turns and goes back to his red cabin, quick as he can.

Years later, when Isaiah had returned to Samuel's Bay and he was noting it all down – so that she could know something of the truth – Isaiah came to see how those years in the city were nothing but an illusion. Isaiah walked the streets and he wove the silk and he played at poker and he sat and watched the river – but all he did in fact was hide. He hid from his weakness, he hid from his fear. He hid from the truth that his arrival here in the city was not predestined, it was only another part of running away. He hid from the danger of the strike and he did not even take the opportunity to make friends once more with all the old people. His loneliness was due to circumstance but it was also a choice, an elected part of his existence – and it was only years later, it was only then when he was going over it all in his mind, trying to reconstruct the past, that he saw he chose it for ease. He chose it because he was afraid that if he connected with people, with life once more, he might be as hurt as he had been when Comfort and Ezekiel died, when Athene Brown was born and he was forced to grow up all at once.

But now self-knowledge for Isaiah is as elusive as years before were the fish in Samuel's Bay. Now Isaiah lurks in his cabin, waiting for things to improve. He returns to talk to the young man but each time the arguments are paraded before him, he remains recalcitrant, clinging only to their encounters in the hope that things will go back to how they were. He goes to seek out Frank Armstrong, to wander back to the den and play a hand or two – but when he reaches Frank's place, he hears the voices of all the others, the Ivys and the Rons, and it is too much, they all seem to come as a package.

Months go by and as Isaiah finds himself discomfited, so the discontent in the warehouses grows. The young man's ardour does not seem to diminish – not in the face of the stubbornness of the warehouse owners, not in the face of the bad weather or the increasingly hard-pressed workforce. Each time there is a setback, Isaiah sees how the young man wins them round. Rouses them with his passion and his glinting eyes. Rouses them because ThisisWhatisRight.

Sometimes Isaiah even finds himself nodding in agreement. For want of something else to do, he might go to a meeting, stand at the back and the murmur that runs through the workers will catch him, somehow, unawares.

Isaiah himself has developed a cough – his lungs are no longer lungs of the sea, lungs of hot winds, salt air, and he wonders for an instant, perhaps there is justice in the cause, perhaps this should be stopped.

But then he hears that they are planning a climax and instinctively Isaiah wants to open his mouth, he wants to put out his hand and stop the young man, stop, this is too much. Isaiah does not understand his own fears but they are tangible now and he does not want this to happen, he is sure of that. He loves his work. He loves the warehouse and the cobwebs in the roof that are laced with rainbows and the rickety-rack, clickety-clack. He loves the silence and the noise. He loves his humdrum thip-thap routine – stepping out down the streets, along the river, over the mudflat; leaving his hat on a hook while he listens to Kitty someone, leaving his hat on another while he puts his head down, works on his loom.

Isaiah hides from the plans but they find him all the same. There is going to be a strike. There is going to be a Big Day. Months of paralysis will be solved by the Big Day. They will march up and along, past the river, past the church, under the bridge, into the heart of the town. The young man says they will shout out their grievances. They will meet with others who will agree with them, who will reinforce their argument. They will be heard – by the leaders of the town, leaders of the country, and everyone will be forced to agree that this is what should be done. Isaiah feels the young man shake him warmly by the hand as they sit on their barrels and the plans fall smartly into place.

*　　*　　*

And then one day at dawn, when the rains are easing, when the Big Day looms large, when Isaiah has been away from Samuel's Bay for twenty years and all the recent crises seem to be coming to a head, Isaiah goes to the deep-dark ribbon of the river, sits on his creel, watches time flowing by.

And he sees her. Or he thinks it is her. There is a group of them. They are strangers, brought in by the warehouse owners to do the work. Their faces are unfamiliar to Isaiah, the way they walk unfamiliar also. Isaiah's heart sinks when he sees them, he knows what it means. He knows that no matter what the young man says, the battle is being lost.

They are mostly men. Some of them are old but a few are young. They have faces burnt hard by the sun. Among them, the odd woman. And at the very back, a younger one, girl almost – and she wears a carving, could it be a fish, about her neck. She wears a felt cloche hat enlaced with beads that dances on her head like a moonbeam. Around her wrist, a cowrie-shell bracelet. Around her waist, a scarf embroidered with sequins, embroidered with patterns of the sea.

Isaiah feels the weight of his past come tumbling down upon him.

In all his time in the town, in all his wanderings, Isaiah had not been to the boatyard. At first he had not dared to come. He had a secret fear – inadmissible perhaps – that he might come here and it would be too close to the sea. He would smell the salt, hear the roar, the crash, the blue and Samuel's Bay might call him back or drag him back. Then slowly Isaiah came to see that he did not need to go. He saw the sea was only for fishermen and Isaiah was a townsman now, man among many. He saw that the river was gentler, kinder, that sitting on his creel was as far as he need travel.

But today Isaiah has come, quaking, to the boatyard. He is bristling with panic. The wind-up gramophone plays unheard, Isaiah's bed remains unmade, the door on his red cabin blows in the wind and through the mud of the dark broad bog that was once the mudflat, you can see the deeper footsteps of a running man.

How many weeks is it since he saw the girl he thought might be Athene Brown? Isaiah cannot count because his whole being is overcome with horror. At nights he has tried to sleep but now his cough has worsened and his ribs are goading him with pain. He has tried to banish the picture of her from his mind because he had thought she was dead. He has tried to lull himself back into the solace of routine but at dawn, when he goes to the warehouse, he finds the gates are closed this time – no silk today, no workers today.

Then he thought he would find her again, he would find that girl with the carved fish around her neck and the bead-encrusted hat on her head and the small tackle-bag across her shoulder – and he would show himself that he had not seen Athene Brown, that the girl he saw was someone else. So Isaiah has run in and out of the cats' cradle of the town – up the streets, down the streets. Into the church, out of the church, into the warehouses and out, quickly, again because Isaiah is both eager to find her and afraid.

He has run – like the dogs with no hair, the dogs with hair – in and out of the market stalls, ignoring the mud on his shins and the wet in his bones, ignoring his cough, ignoring the shouts hey you because for the first time since he has been here, Isaiah is noticed; and he wants it to be finished business, he wants to revert to those creel-sitting days and he can flow towards his death like the river. But he does not find her; and he does not find anyone who knows about the strangers he saw; he does not find anyone who knows the name Athene Brown and he has to stop because there is almost nowhere else for him to go.

And one day at last, Isaiah runs down to the river mouth. He dares to run to the fringe of the sea, into the boatyard. Tucked in between the jetties and the warehouses and the staircases that seem to lead to nowhere, between big boats and barges, little boats and here it is, where they all come to rest and whence they all go out to sea.

A light burns in the shed window – it is late, it is dark. Isaiah moves towards the shed. Ropes and canvas and bits of wood spill out onto the foreshore. Isaiah feels an old frisson. Inside, floats and jibs and hawsers and bungs hang suspended from the roof. Isaiah pushes his way in. There is a stitching machine. There is thread, there are needles and widgets and rivets and huge spreads of cloth. Isaiah clears his throat, he calls helloo-o, he gazes at the drawings spread out on a table.

Isaiah is bristling with panic because he needs to go back. They have closed the silk factory and the detail he could hide in has once again been wrested from his grasp. His red hut is marooned in a swamp and Isaiah has summoned up the ghosts of his past and in a flash, it has come to him, he never saw her die, he never saw her dead; and now he has seen her again, she was walking in the streets with a young man Isaiah thought he recognised and Isaiah is afraid now, sleepless, hopeless . . . He has tried to ask the gods what he should do, he has tried to find that girl, he has tried to scourge fear of the future with a blank ellipsis of the past – but he knows he must go.

If she is there, he says to himself, I will go up and embrace her, I will go up and beg her forgiveness. If she is there, we will come back here to the town, we will be happy, all will be repaired. If she is there, we might cast out a line for old times' sake, we might row out the boat for old times' sake, we might stay awhile – but then we will come back because now, this is where I belong.

If she is not there, he says to himself, she will be nowhere. If Samuel's Bay is empty, I will know that she died in the storm, that I was right, the gods were cruel. If she is not there, I will plant a cross on Lion Rock, I will stow my heart on Lion Rock and the sea will know she has been, they will know her passing has been marked.

Isaiah hums this as a mantra to himself while he asks the man from the boatyard if he can build a boat. Isaiah's thoughts are noisy and he makes his request but he does not notice the effect of his words and he does not wait to hear the answer. The man who owns the boatyard is standing on his threshold. He has a pipe in his mouth and he is sucking deep and the river is calm now, the man stands quietly.

Isaiah asks the man again because he was not paying attention, because he did not hear the response. Outside, among the detritus of the yard, there lies a half-built hull. There is a hammer on the ground, there are nails and Isaiah knows what he can do, he can sail back to his birdoflove, he can find her back in Samuel's Bay – dead or alive he does not care, he will plant her a cross on Lion Rock and then he will return.

And Isaiah speaks to the boatyard man, under the cool moon, by the sleeping river, waiting again for a reply.

Isaiah immerses himself in his project and he forgets the passage of time. Days turn into nights and Isaiah is driven, he does not see any other way or any other plan but the plan to build a boat, the plan to go back to Samuel's Bay. Strikes rage on in the town; a swell of angry voices courses through the streets but Isaiah is driven, Isaiah does not hear. He works for the boatman and in his spare time he builds a boat for himself. He works all day and his bones are heavy with fatigue but Isaiah is a man, he does not have to tie himself to anyone, he ignores the pull of his muscles and presses on. If he sleeps, it is for an hour or two and he snatches it, curled up in a sail. If he eats, it is bread; if he drinks, it is water and he does not notice how it tastes or whether it fills him, only he pushes on with his building and he sees nothing, no one else.

In years to come, Athene Brown will try to picture her father as he worked to build a boat. Did he sit there in the boatyard, whisper birdoflove to himself as he beat the panels and caulked the planks? Did he squat down beneath the curved bottom of his boat and wonder what on earth he was doing, why on earth he was driving himself so hard? Years later, she found the boatman and she heard how Isaiah had pushed himself to the very edge of sanity. His sleep became delirious, his words became garbled, his actions were robotic and almost frightening because he was so caught up in the urgency and necessity of his plan.

She heard how he built not one boat, but two – one for the boatman and one for himself because that was their agreement. And she heard too, when the last nail was banged, when the last screw was turned and the last plank set fair, that the boatman asked Isaiah why are you doing this why have you worked so what is it that makes you push yourself to the limits of endurance. And Isaiah had turned to the boatman – mopping up the last bead of sweat, rubbing the last raw blister from the palm of his hand – and he had said I have done it for love.

Because I danced in the waters of love.

The boat resembles the one Ezekiel died in, when it was smashed upon the Deadmen. It has a cabin and a sail and a jib and it is strong and sturdy but small. The man who owns the boatyard has watched as it has grown from a few sticks into a sea-going vessel. The man smokes on his pipe. He sits on a thick block of oak that has been washed up in one of the storms. Business is not so good and he is pleased Isaiah has come because now that that half-built boat has been finished, it is ready to sell.

The boatyard man watches as Isaiah sets to to push the new boat off its ways. Isaiah has to push like a madman. Groans issue from his whip-like frame. Sweat seeps from his forehead. At one point, the boatyard man believes he is going to have to put down his pipe, to get up and lend the man a hand because goodness knows, it is hard enough to watch so much effort go unrewarded. Then there is a creak and a grind. Isaiah has set it on its way at last.

The boatyard man watches as the boat eases down its tracks. He watches as it takes its place on the water, as Isaiah leapfrogs over the side and there is a flurry of ropes. He watches as the thin dark sickly man assumes his place at the helm. He watches as the water licks up the side, darkening the red paint as it goes. He watches the sails unfurl and he hears a small hoot from its hooter and there is a brilliant glittering sunset tonight, crisp, black, ochre, tangerine.

The boatyard man sucks on his pipe while the small red boat disappears into the flat burning plain of the sea.

Part Three

One

Athene Brown is heading towards the town. She is leaving the battered huts, the rotting boats, the bay. You see her as she walks up over the ridge. She has thick curling hair that bobs up and down on her back. She has dark sunned skin and she walks with purpose. Every now and again she pauses, bends down – perhaps to examine a snail or a plant, you cannot be sure. Or she pauses and she turns round, sucks in the view of the sea that has always rolled out in a lapping mauve counterpane before her.

On her back, Athene carries a small pack – inside, there is the fossil of a fish, a coloured stone; there are one or two costumes, there is a shell-embedded mirror, an old encyclopaedia and, besides, there is a book of pressed flowers, one of many that she found in his hut after he died. This one she has chosen because it smells of his cheroots; because each of its pages contains a flat agapanthus, frail like a butterfly's wing; because somehow he has kept alive their colour yet preserved their skeletal beauty and she reads in each of them an exacted promise that she return to Samuel's Bay.

*   *   *

How did she feel on that morning when she woke and saw the two Johnnies had gone? When she found herself alone in the bay, at last?

What was it that woke her? Athene was thick with sleep and grief and at first she could not fathom why she had woken so, with a start. Was it the banging? There must be a wind. What was it banging? And where were the old men? Where was their coughing, their whining? All those tetchy her-herms which they started to let out first thing so she would have to get up because they were hungry or they were anxious or they wanted her attention, only they did not know why.

The wind blew in through her window and the banging went on. The wind was hot and Athene Brown got up from her bed which was too small now. She shouted out Hello-o. She waited for an answer but there was none and she thought maybe it was just that her voice had been swallowed in all that noise. She dressed slowly. She wrapped a sequin cloth around her hair. She squinted in the mirror, rubbed her tired green eyes. She put a cowrie-shell bracelet on her wrist, she stepped out onto her veranda – slowly, because it was only seven days and eight nights since he had died. She looked about, at first blinded by the bright morning sun and she had to blink in the wind too. She went to go to Dublin's hut – to wake the old boys, to talk to the old boys, to ooo-arr about the wind and hear her own voice and theirs and feel better for having shared this momentary unease.

And then she saw that Dublin's door was flapping, that the noise was the bang-bang because they had forgotten to latch it behind them. And her heart thumped like a beating drum because she knew the truth – at once.

If they had given her a chance, she could have gone with them. She could have chased them as they left her that morning, begged them not to leave her, thrown stones at their backs as they rushed on away from her because how could they be so selfish, thoughtless. She could have shouted at them as they went how it was not that bad; she could have showed them how they were only making a mistake, how one grief was leading them to another, how they were leaving a place they knew for somewhere they would never know; she could have screamed out he is still here – listen and you will hear him, listen and you will hear the old ghosts, they have not gone.

Athene climbed the Lion Rock. She sat on its tip with her arms wrapped round her knees and her sequin scarf blowing out to sea. Tears did not come. Rage did not come. There were no words for who would hear them? There was no cry because all moisture had drained from her mouth. Her lips stuck to her teeth and Athene Brown stayed there for hours or days, she would be hard pressed to say how long. She was alone and the wind sang its songs only to her. The fish who would flee the bay need not be so afraid now, there was only her. Leaves blew and this was unusual here but Athene Brown did not pick them up, only she sat and watched them as they swirled in eddies at her feet.

Then she was numb. She meandered from the Rock to the hut to the shore in a clouded, woolly, circular process that meant nothing, not then while she was doing it, not years later when she looked back. Separate emotions assailed her – fear, at nights; hunger, most of the time. There was rain. There were storms. The wind blew the door off her hut and she was obliged to take shelter in Dublin's – where the two Johnnies and the old bugger had lived together for so many years – and she felt like an interloper, trespassing on their shadows.

One day Athene walked up behind the bay to pick some agapanthus. There were not many flowers for some reason, perhaps the winds had been too strong, but at last she found one, tucked deep into a groove in the rock. Athene snapped the stem, low down, near the root. She let the sap ooze over her fingers and the wind whip her hair and the sand stick to her lips and she remembered that day, her sixth birthday when she had done the same with Isaiah, when they had both staggered down from the top, laden with flowers. She remembered how he would not answer her, how he would not tell her his plan and it had been a day of surprise and they had laughed together, only he must have known even then that inside there was another plan.

They had all gone. They had all left her, one way or another. They had kept their secrets and they had let them worm holes inside them and they had left her, as though she did not matter, as though life was so simple, you could just get up, walk away.

And yet she survived. She struggled through her incomprehension. She found that her past was cruel, it ambushed her when she least sought it out. But she found too that the past was kind, its edges blurred, the detail faded. Where once every day she longed for her father, now she found she could barely recall his face. Where every day she had enjoyed the old men – their grumbling, wretched bloody wind, cussed bloody sand – now she found that the matter of life, it took her over, filled in the gaps.

She sat on the rocks – still as a heron – and waited for a tiny fish to wriggle past. She swam in the shallows when the tide was out, scouring the pools or the seabed for any form of edible life. She walked up to the ridge and picked the fruit, she walked out to the well and brought in the water, she mended the rope, she beat down the planks, she clung to life.

In the evenings, when she had gathered in wood and lit a fire, Athene examined the things that had washed up that day on the shore – the trinkets and old bones and shells of brilliant colours. She sorted them into piles on the veranda – blue stones, green stones, brown shells, orange shells – and the boarding round her hut gleamed in a bumpy rainbow. Sometimes she stole into Dublin's and brought out his old books that were filled with pressed flowers. Some of the flowers had been tinted and all were preserved in a state which was not natural and yet was exquisitely eloquent, telling in each perfect specimen the story of the wonder of nature, telling the story of Dublin Small's enduring love for his land.

Or she did not do anything but instead she sat still, let her eyes close, let the past such as she felt it come back to her – memories of her bright-garden days with Isaiah, of the walks that they took and the knowledge of plants and insects and weather that he shared with her as they went; those days when they swam out together in the sea, when she lay on the cup of his chest as he lay on his back and they floated, soft sea-breeze lifting their hair; those days when they fished together, when he took her out big boat small boat and he let her hold a hook on a string on a stick over her prow and see what she could catch; days when they just sat, maybe out on their veranda, maybe up in the cutty-grass clearing, when she was there and he was behind her and they looked out, over the bright sea.

Athene had learnt the bay as a child but now as she grew into a woman, she learnt it again. She learnt the changing patterns, as then she had learnt the points that remained fixed. She learnt how the sun could shine and the wind blow and the rain fall all at once while a double set of rainbow hoops jumped up from the sea. She sat from time to time on the top of the Lion Rock and watched how the shadows of clouds could dance in the waves; how the waves could distort the shadows into pictures of people she thought she had known, into words she thought she had heard. She turned round to face the land and she could sit there for hours, days at a time – listen to the wind as it rattled through the flax, watch the sea as it chewed into the dunes.

So that slowly there came a rhythm. Slowly, slowly the pieces fell into her heart – as she picked up the encyclopaedia and dreamt over the words, the pictures, the places; as she battled with storms and fought with hunger; as she tended the fish or left the fish, as she repaired one of the last sound boats and she learnt to navigate the Deadmen. She became a rugged swimmer and her lithe, brown, whipping limbs took her all over the bay – even as far as the island where they went that time to pick mussels. She watched the minke mother and her calf, as the calf grew and then there was another. She watched the albatrosses soar, she watched the dark slicks of seaweed, she sat on a rocky atoll miles away from the bay and looked back and thought she would never know anything more proud, more strong than the Lion Rock.

One day Athene Brown picked up a knife. A turtle had been swept up dead on the beach. There were sad eyes and a gnarled wise unspeaking face and there was tortoiseshell and flesh and Athene Brown held the shell up to the sun, let the light shimmer through, mottling the sand. Her mind ran back to the day of the fish-storm, sitting on his lap, clinging on to him. She began to carve. She ran the knife on its edge or on its point. She pressed and she squeezed, she moulded and she scraped. A small fish began to emerge from the carving.

She would spend hours perfecting it. Hours rubbing it, honing it, trying to make the fish in the exact image she carried in her mind. Sometimes she would start again – maddened because what she envisaged and what she held in her hand were miles apart. Perhaps it was the eyes that eluded her. Or the mouth. Perhaps it was just the scale of the fish, its proportions. She gave up. She started again. She took another piece of shell, she began another fish-carving and this cycle of imagination-versus-product, it tormented her because she had glimpses of what she wanted to achieve and long spells where nothing seemed to be right.

She came to find out what she could do. There was energy and she channelled it. There were thoughts and she followed them. There was incredible stubbornness and this she hung on to because she was alone. There was her red hut and she filled it, layering every surface with objects that shimmered or glittered, objects that sang or glowed or just made her belong because somehow she was always afraid she might be made to leave. There were long days which ended when she was exhausted, when her arms and legs could not move another inch. There were longer days still, when she could do nothing because the wind pinned her inside her hut – and these hung heavy and sometimes she would sit, listen to the sea-chimes, wonder where on earth this was all going to lead.

She stayed here because she knew nowhere else; she survived because she chose life. She developed a resilience and a freedom of spirit that enveloped her, a hard carapace – like that of the turtle – and it shut out all regret for the past, embraced only the present.

How many times over those years did Athene wake and think her presence here was not desired? The weather was cruel and she often went hungry. The seasons were cruel and they tested her endurance, sometimes to the very limits – with their hot winds and their droughts, with their plagues of insects or their hut-destroying deluges of rain. Winds tried to blow her off the Lion Rock. Waves tried to drown her in the sea, tried to suck her boat down, then smash it on the Deadmen. Days yawned out ahead of her when she could do nothing, and Athene Brown might want to climb the

Rock or mount the ridge but she could not – the gales were too fierce – and she was obliged to sit inside her hut with her noisy thoughts, no one beside her to hear their echo.

She went over the arguments time and again in her mind: every time the door blew off her hut or the chimney came down; every time she had to scramble up onto the roof, cutting her legs on the tin, because with no flue her hut filled with smoke and where was the pleasure in that. Where would she go? She knew nothing. There was the town. There were the open valleys that spread beyond, there was the sea. There was the big turquoise cup of the sky and she could be free. She could find comfort, humanity, food in the town, perhaps she might even find the two Johnnies. Perhaps it would be no harder in the open valleys or the open sea but she knew nothing and the sky that did not look down on Samuel's Bay seemed so big somehow, too big.

Her fears were tamed here. She had grown used to the boundaries of the bay, to her solitude, to the storms. She knew the place like a blind man, she groped its contours. She knew the dunes and if the winds were fierce and they changed, she knew them again because she became used to the patterns they chose, to their habits.

And then she had found something here – as the pieces fell into the jigsaw of her heart. She had found a mission. Something to ease the itch of her fingers in the morning, to keep them working through the day: she would save the bay. She would bring the fish back to Samuel's Bay and so she would save it – at least in the eyes of the legend.

Athene knew the story of Samuel because who did not. She knew that in its kinder versions, he was attributed with the lushness of the bay, with the richness of the stocks. He above all had helped to make the bay so fecund, so rich in fish. In his small way, Samuel was a king. Those who had followed him scorned his work and Athene Brown, who did not wish to think how her own family had disappointed her, thought instead of the legend. She thought of the way in which her people, her forebears, had destroyed his work in barely one generation – fickle with treasure, as though it grew out of the mists. She saw him, one man, responsible for this alone – and she thought I will do it also.

Athene Brown dressed as a man of the sea and she did all she could to encourage the fish to return. She made notes in her mind of places where fish seemed slowly to be returning in any number and she did not catch them, only she allowed them be. She learnt the spawning season and she learnt to identify the females and she learnt the habits of the shoals because there was no point, she understood that much, in letting the same mistakes be made again. She tried to find and protect their beds. She tried to ward off their predators and as she did so she tried to tiptoe through the waters, more and more like a fish herself so that they did not sense that the source of their demise had returned.

It was ill thought out. It was ill understood and Athene had a sense that she was blowing vain words onto the winds and they would barely listen because when do the gods listen to a child like her. It was ill fated and often she came and she found that her efforts had been destroyed, a female was dead or they were all dead and maybe it was too late now, the damage had been done. Athene Brown got up at dawn, she collapsed into bed at dusk and she was driven by her one-woman mission to restore Samuel's Bay to its old status as an Eden filled with fish.

At times she would be swamped with despair. How could she make a difference, how could she save the bay, single-handed? How could years of greed and devastation be undone by one girl in one lifetime? She remembered the story that Dublin had told her of the man who built a forest; who collected the acorns and all the nuts of all the trees and slowly, over his lifetime, restored a barren valley to somewhere filled with water, greenness, grace. Athene Brown had no grand plan. She barely thought she would succeed – how could she be so bold, so naïve? But she was half-child and she could still summon up that rage – black-and-white childish indignation – that swept over her during the fish-storm because something was wrong and something had to be put right.

And moreover she was half-woman and she was finding her own strength. She had resilience, endurance, the pattern of her life had seen to that. She was fierce sometimes, steely. There was no one to help her, she had to succeed. She would stand in the sand pulling the boat or lugging a rock or digging a hole and her muscles would scream and her back would scream and her mind would say I cannot do this – but she did it, because she had to. Half-woman, she was finding out what she could do.

Perhaps the seasons were right, perhaps she should leave. Perhaps it was hopeless, a girl alone, pitting herself against the elements. But Athene Brown held on to her stubbornness, her steeliness, and she clung to her mission. She would be satisfied only when she had made some tiny mark; when she had spilt some drops of her blood in the sand between her toes; when she had proved after all that she was something, someone; when she had proved to herself – because who else was there – that it was all right, to survive on your own. And maybe, further than that, someone somewhere would know she had been. Maybe her work would reach out and her deeds would speak for her and maybe someone some time would know that she was worth something, that she had lived. Athene Brown needed to fulfil her mission because this was where she belonged, in Samuel's Bay. She owed a debt – to the gods perhaps, to the bay undoubtedly, to the shameful memory of those who had been and taken all they could.

One day – she said to herself, as she fought with cold, with heat, as she swam through storms, as she battled with the elements, as she laboured ill fated against all the odds – one day again, she would climb to the height of the Lion Rock and she would see a necklace of fish. It would string through the water, trailing in its wake a gentle lightning. She would stroll through the water and feel the snaking of thousands and thousands of fins against her calves. She would roll her head back on her shoulders, she would laugh, she would sing out . . .

If the winds were trying to drive Athene Brown to leave, there were others too. In the daytime, she was busy and she worked hard and for the most part she felt right in all that she did. She was tested – and she survived.

122

But at night, also, Athene Brown found she was pursued. Her sleep was peppered with dreams. She lay down exhausted but thick deep rest was only brief. Soon the ghosts of her past – all the people she had known – came flooding into her unconscious. There was Dublin Small – Athene lay there eyes closed and her nose twitched at the smell of his cheroot smoke. He took various forms – sometimes he was made of nothing but letters B U G G E R; sometimes he was an old bear with a wound, sometimes an ancient man, close to death, no flesh.

The two Johnnies came also – they came as one or as two. They came as they were in their early days and they were separate, distinguishable and she saw them teaching her things, talking to her; they came later, when Dublin had died, and they had fused. She saw their backs as they hobbled off over the sand dunes. She saw their twin pairs of boots lined up by their bed, because in their anxiety to leave, they had run away barefoot.

The ghosts of the village – the Cuckeltys, the Normans, Ivy Peacock, even old Samuel himself – seemed to have chosen her as their meeting place. They toyed with her. They rattled out ideas and they paraded themselves as caricatures, embodiments of good and bad and there was always running, running here, running away and Athene Brown would wake in the mornings exhausted, troubled.

And then there was Isaiah. Isaiah came. Not often at first, she would not allow it, she shut her mind to him dead or alive. She blotted out her first seven years and the thought of where he might be and if he threatened to appear to her, she would wake up or roll over or get up.

But then slowly she let him come and his back too was always turned to her. She could not see his face. She could not remember his face either – awake or in dreams. She saw his thin body and his dark shoulders. She saw a fishing rod or a boat or a net. She would waken – when Isaiah had been – and have to fetch some water, wipe it over her eyes and her forehead, because otherwise the sweat would make her itch.

Isaiah became a more frequent visitor. She would wake up and think he had been calling to her. She would wake up and feel an echo in her mind of a man crying out and she would be afraid that it was Isaiah, locked in despair. She would find herself watching great pictographic scenes where a man in his boat fought wide open seas – a man tiny, his boat tiny, the swell huge and foaming and the boat would disappear from sight beneath a wall of water and Athene would find herself gripped with fear, tension, panic because she could not see him, she was not sure what had happened.

The years went by and the scenes developed. There was more tension in the dreams, more terror about Isaiah's fate, and Athene grew a palpable sense of her father, each time she looked out to sea. She came to believe that her inner life was no more than a reflection of her real world. Maybe these were not dreams but memories? She pictured him – when she was not absorbed in her work, fighting the winds, struggling to save the fish – and he was always at odds with nature, in trouble. She became so caught up in the drama of her secrets that she could not entertain another fate for Isaiah and she only saw

124

him, his back turned towards her, disappearing beneath the sea.

It evolved subtly into a burden of guilt. From seeing him in trouble on the water, she saw that somehow she was to blame for his leaving her. She remembered bright-garden days and then he had run away. Perhaps she was always ill fated. Perhaps she drew the wrath of the gods and they visited it on those around her. After all they had taken Dublin Small, they had chased away the two Johnnies. Perhaps Athene was a magnet for ill fortune and she had been a child maybe but she had driven him away – how, she could not be sure.

Exhaustion fought with a fear of sleep. Athene Brown pursued relentlessly the goals of her mission during the daytime and at night she tossed and turned on her too-small bed while she tried to reconstruct those first seven years, while she tried to comprehend just what it was that she had done to chase him out of her life.

Soon she dreaded his coming in her dreams because it was too much. She came to accept the burden of guilt but she did not wish to watch him over and over again as he appeared to be sucked down into the waves. She longed for Dublin Small, whom she had loved unconditionally. She longed even for the two Johnnies because there was solace in their pettiness. She longed for the days when Isaiah talked to her, when he held her in his lap and told her of his birdoflove, told her of Comfort and their days of delirious joy together.

And as she thought of Comfort, Athene Brown would seem to close in on the truth of her guilt. It was as though there, in the death of her mother, there lay an answer. Isaiah had never expressed regret to her, he had never blamed her – but Athene Brown was afraid that perhaps after all that was it. That she had killed his only love when she had been born. Athene came and she took Comfort away.

Athene's days descended into haze. She barely slept at night, she worked herself to her very nerve ends while there was light and she could no longer think clearly. The distinctions between her imaginary world and the real one were so blurred that Athene sometimes wondered whether she was alive or dead, whether she too was not just another phantom.

And just as she struggled to reconcile her living moments with her imagined ones, so Athene struggled in her mission. The fish were not returning. It did not matter what she did or how successful her efforts appeared to be, Athene saw no change in the stocks of the bay, no improvement in the number or the incidence of shoals. There were dead fish sometimes but mostly there were no fish. The beds that she sought to protect remained empty.

Dreams overflowed into her daytime and Athene began to make mistakes. Distracted, she chased away any fish that she found. Or she caught them; or she forgot to put them back quickly enough or she forgot to put them back at all. She knew that things were slipping from her and she tried to claw them back. She dressed in many disguises. She took the role of a fish herself but it made no difference, she could not hide from the truth that her work was not coming any closer to fruition. Isaiah was a constant presence – he was saying you to her You You; You You as he fought on the water, You You as his boat was swallowed by the surf and she did not see him any longer, and one day Athene Brown found herself giving up – on it all. On the bay, on the fish, on the sleepless nights and the wind damn-you-wind on the Lion Rock on the sea on it all and she sat down on the floor of her hut and she just sat down.

And she picked up a small tackle-bag. She ran her finger in a pattern on the sand-strewn floor, drew absent-mindedly the picture of a stickleback.

And she picked up one or two items. She ran her mind over the contours of a minke whale.

And she put them inside. She heard in her head the song of the chimes which rang then and always with the sound of the sea.

And she knew that she was going to leave – after all this time. She stood up and let the door bang to behind her.

She walks with purpose. It is hard, after all this time, to lose that urgency. Her hair bobs on her back and the sun strokes her dark brown skin. Today is a kind day. The sky is high and there is no wind. The grassy coat on the Lion Rock does not ruffle and there is no fringe on the waves and the leaves on the flax bushes do not rustle. Suck in your chest and it is fresh, this air. Roll your head back on your neck and you will feel grand, proud, alive.

Athene Brown keeps her head down and her chest empty. She does not know where she is going quite or why. She fingers the stickleback round her neck and she feels the pack as it knocks her on the spine but she does both unconsciously. Is she following the ghosts of her dreams? Is she running away from them? Is she leading them out of the chaos of Samuel's Bay to somewhere new where they might just leave her alone? Right now Athene Brown does not care. She is running because she needs to but she is deeply saddened that this is all she can do. She is giving up on her mission. How can she do that, how can she give up on Samuel's Bay? How can she leave the fish and not be sure that they are going to return?

Today is a kind day and Athene climbs up onto the ridge. You can smell the scent of ripe apples but Athene does not pick one. There is thyme under her feet, rich and pungent, but she does not smile. Along the pathways, as she moves further away from the bay, there are flowers she has not seen before, there are plants subtly different from the ones she has known. Dublin Small would have been intrigued to see them: miniature pink-flowering cacti with fat succulent leaves, tiny blue orchids clinging to their stems. The ridge opens out and now you are above the sea, moving in a straight line across the headland. The trees are behind you and here it is like tundra, open plain. The flora clings to the ground – no longer showy but timid – because here, when the wind comes, there are no rocks to break its passage.

Athene trudges on. Occasionally she bends down – to look at a bug or a plant – but it is vague only, her interest. Or she turns round, from time to time, to take another last look at the sea. She takes her bag off her back and grips it to her chest. She is dressed as Athene Brown today but there are one or two costumes in her pack, just in case. She does not know what is in store for her and she can barely remember what it is that she leaves behind and her mind echoes with the song of the chimes because they are hanging in her hut, ringing then and always with the sound of the sea.

Two

The plain stretches out behind her and the counterpane of the sea is far in the distance. There is a crick thwack from her bag where her few possessions are knocking together but now Athene Brown is looking ahead. Years of footprints have brought her here – footpaths from the bay to the town with the steps of the Cuckeltys and the Normans, Ivy Peacock, the two Johnnies ingrained in the earth, part of them. Without making a plan, Athene Brown has followed their trail. Perhaps she wishes to find the two Johnnies. Perhaps curiosity has driven her because here after all is where they all went.

The town feathers into the plain and it is hard to know where it begins. With the back of a cabin? With the hint of a smell of cooking? With a scrap of food or the margins of the bounds of a hairless dog? Athene Brown is moving from one era to the next, from one landscape to another. Dust greets her from the dirt-dust streets. Noise builds slowly in her consciousness. Athene looks up at the sky and it is the same rich blue but she lowers her gaze and everything is changed. The roar of the sea has become the grand unfurling honky-tonk of the river. The moan of the wind has become the rush of the water, the push of the barges, the screech of the birds chasing the day's catch in the nets, the man-din, rope-noise, shouts, you-do-this. Faces swoon up to meet her, brown faces, yellowing faces, faces with teeth and faces with no teeth. Faces that are isolated and more often faces that merge into the chaos of newness, grinning or glowering, chattering or angrily wrapped in their own hostile cloak of silence.

Athene Brown stops, perches on an old creel. Perhaps to bring her back to a world she understands, she opens her bag.

Though she cannot know it, today is the Big Day. Today the plans of the young man have cemented and Athene Brown has arrived as the thick crocodile of silk-weavers rocks-and-rolls its way towards the heart of the town.

From above, you could look down and see the creature – this crocodile – as it lumbers its way, sinuous, from the town's extremities to its gut. There are plumes of dust trailing out behind. Granules of matter – sweat, dirt, hope – climb up into the air, then drop down again, to cling on to its slick Big-Day coat. The creature is clumsy yet somehow graceful. It keeps its head high. It keeps its steps in time. Pride courses through its veins because today for once the creature is not a beast of burden.

At the head of the group, the young man walks and he too feels his heart bursting with pride. Today all those words become deeds, all those promises come closer to fulfilment.

The young man feels tall. His smart Big-Day clothes are itchy but he pays no attention.

Athene Brown rummages through her bag and she does not hear the rising swell of noise, she does not sense the increasing thickness of the air. She is too close still to her recent dramas, to the loss of those she has loved, to the disappointment she feels in giving up on Samuel's Bay. Athene picks over her belongings – flicks through the old encyclopaedia, picks-up-puts-down a piece of a costume, glances in her shell-embedded mirror. Maybe in doing this, she is giving herself more time, withdrawing once more into the cocoon of her story . . .

. . . but today, of all days, the workers have no time to wait. They are marching towards Triumph and Reward and Vindication. They have come round a corner and now they flank the river and their eyes look forwards, paying attention only to their mute determination, to the rising swell of Rightness that flows through their veins. Rightness presses the steps ever forwards. Rightness makes them warm, proud, urgent and the tension that was embodied earlier in shifting feet and grumbling stomachs is changing, converting itself into rage and hurry. Unexpectedly, the young man finds himself slipping from his position at the fore.

The old men who chew on their baccy, who sit on upturned barrels, who have come out once more because today holds plenty of promise, they turn round to look at the growing noise. See the mouths and eyes, hot breath, heads and faces and pinafores and feet, stamping feet. See the young man as he breaks into a jog; see the young man as he turns round, running backwards, so he can face his men. Dissect the shouts that merge into one circling cry, wewantmorepay, wewantmorepay, booming down the street, along the river, under the bridge, in and out of the cabin shops. See the girl sitting on the creel, her buttocks pressing in small squares through the mesh. See her with her head down as she delves through her belongings. See how she does not seem to decipher any change in the roll of city-noise, only holds up a shell-embedded mirror, tracing the map of her smile, the map of her grass-dark eyes, the fall of her hair, twisty with dust. Admire the glints of her sequin-layered scarf, the soft round warm shape of the cowrie shells that dance on her wrist. Half-woman looking back and they watch open-mouthed how she does not notice anything, not the footsteps coming closer, not the air becoming thicker, not the bass-note drone of a crowd that is about to roll over the top of her . . .

There is a sooty, musty smell. There are motes of matter hanging in the air. She looks up because she is lying on her back and the roof is not so high, she can see the cobwebs festooned with coloured fibres and Athene Brown closes her eyes again because it is safer, easier. Where is she? Athene looks into the amber of her eyelids and imagines there is a soft red wind and a light smattering of grains of sand and she imagines some strangers' arms reaching down towards her as she lies there.

Can she remember what has just happened? Can she recall the shunt as the young man collided with her, with the creel, as both bodies hit the earth and the dust jumped up to embrace them? Can she remember the silence, *huurgh*, bated breath, the scrunch as all the feet stopped, then the hum soft this time that went through the crowd because there on the ground was a girl glittery colourful stranger lying unconscious?

Athene Brown feels a shadow pass over her. The amber turns to beige. There is a sound, rustling of lips, murmuring. She does not hear words specifically, only their resonance. She must open her eyes, she knows that – but first she wants to linger here, in the woozy-amber-musty-smelling haze. The stickleback scratches at her neck.

One era moves to the next, one landscape exchanges itself for another and Athene Brown looks back, weeks later, marvelling at how fast she was swept along. He brought a soft cloth and wiped her face. He brought a soft hand up to the level of her hair and he eased the dusty strands out of her mouth, out of her eyes. She lay woozy on a table and she did not open her eyelids, feeling the dirt being washed from her skin, brushed from her clothes, scraped from her thip-thap feet.

Then there is silence. He leaves her. The noise ebbs, people, footsteps, murmuring easing away. Rainbow dust dances in the cobwebs and Athene Brown listens, hears little – fish, Isaiah, old men, winds, hot-sea sand blending into one long stream of memory.

Later – how many hours later? – he returns. She awakes as the gate of the warehouse compound creaks on its axis. He is alone. He smells tired, no longer slick but crusted with fatigue and spent energy. All the same, he is gentle. As he leans down and peers into the darkness of her closed eyes. As he bends over, puts his arms beneath her, lifts her from the table. As he walks her out, through the yard, through the gate, down early-evening streets.

Sometimes, years later, when she sat once again in the embrace of Samuel's Bay, Athene would dream of the young man who swept that glittering sequin-bedecked sea-exhausted city-shy girl off her feet, who took her back to a place she could never recall, who found in her something she did not know she had. Sometimes Athene Brown would ask herself what might have happened, what turns her story might have taken if there had not been a strike, if she had not sat then on that creel, if she had not undergone at precisely that moment when the silk-weavers arrived on the riverside a seminal and life-shifting realisation as she stared into her shell-embedded mirror.

Tracing the map of her face and for the first time Athene Brown caught a glimpse of her true self. Still half-woman but closer, edging closer to something she would always be. Half-woman but with a core of strength that will define her no matter how hard she may try in the years to come to disguise it. With a resilience, an ability to adapt, a toughness born of experience that may always isolate her. Looking into her grass-dark eyes and the fall of her hair, at her sunburnt cheeks and the steadiness of her gaze, Athene Brown reads her own future, the long ribbon of her life – and at that moment, when the stamping feet of the silk-weavers all but cut it short, she sees the ribbon waving out, alone.

How ironic then that she is bumped into at that exact moment by a young man who seems to know – from the moment he looks at her, lying there unconscious – that all he wants to do is share her solitude; who looks at her and must sense – from her hair? from her passive flickering smile? – a grain of the same scent that he bears, scent of pride perhaps, fierce zeal.

Where does he take her to, that night while her eyes are still closed and he is crusted with fatigue? The air is heavy. Each seems determined to cling on to something a little longer and there are no words, only they listen in secret to one another's breathing. Athene hears the pieces of grit as they wheel off the soles of his Big-Day shoes, one by one. The young man watches as her twisty hair jumps, as her eyelids jolt and the colour in her cheeks ebbs and flows.

He stops to rest. His arms must be tired and he leans against a post of the fence that marks the outer limit of the silk compound. Athene Brown, who has been riven with tension because she is afraid to break the spell – of his gentleness, his tenderness – at last dares to open her eyes . . .

. . . and she stands up now, he lets her down as though she were a crystal vase, he cups a hand beneath her elbow to steady her. She asks stutteringly where's my bag because that is all she has and he pulls it down, he had strung it over his shoulder and he ventures a smile which she can only dimly discern. In the distance the tide of the town is settling into the quiet trance of the night. Athene hears a bell ring. She feels some smoke blow into her nostrils. She sees a man in a vehicle make a dusty rattly crinkling.

Athene Brown paints a portrait of that day, that evening and its colours bleed and merge across her mind's eye. Shadows spread everywhere, seeping down from the church, the warehouses, from the bridge and the box-shaped windowless buildings that litter the far side of the river. The sun cedes to the night and they move side by side, swallowed by chequered darkness.

The long walk and the blur of tears; the footsteps and the orchids and the yawning buff velvet of the open plain; the sea behind, last glimpse of the sea – and in front, the ranks of wooden cabins, lined up in motley rows like children. Snippets of memory: a tramp, old brown coat, heavy gnarled boots, who winks at her as she passes; the old men on their barrels at the side of the river, their lips curled up round dark roots of tobacco; the creel which must have been sat upon before, its top sags and there are one or two gaps in the mesh.

And then, out of nowhere, him. The dark of him. The scent of him. The way he picks her up, the way he breathes over her, she can hear him breathe, she can tell he is kind, she can tell he will love her, care for her – because he does not breathe hard, because he does not push his air into hers. The way he does not walk but seems to glide; the way he bends, the way his shoulders bend, the way his eyes burn and there is a passion there, a fever. The sad pull of his facial muscles, this too enchants her, the way his face is both young and old – responsibility, fever, zeal taking their toll, lending him both gravitas and a hint of something wounded.

Do they go to his cabin house? Where all the faces of his wider family are obliged through lack of space to press together, where the air hums dawn till dusk with words, words, words because here they come to meet – all the militants, all those who wish to see a better working life. Do they go in and out of the wooden shops, through the bazaar, snaking around the pert contiguous clumps of daisies that line the corporation square? Or does he lead her back to the river – all rivers lead to the sea and he takes her hand through streets scattered with the debris of a Big Day, takes her hand down a jetty, down a wooden staircase, down onto the foreshore because this is a tidal river and sometimes here there is space to sit?

He takes off his shoes – as a beautiful, brave gesture towards this unknown barefoot girl, the young man from the city takes off his shoes. He takes off his hat, he lays down her bag, he sweeps her skirt up behind her legs and they sit in the lee of the river wall, their feet trailing in the long grasses which grow among the shingle. Here they are out of the breeze and they sit side by side, gleaming white boy, tawny brown girl.

He asks her her name. There are long pauses while they sit still, while Athene dwells on the tide of sensations sweeping through her and gazes at the river – and then he breaks them with what is your name. And the silence might well up once more because she wants it to slow down, wait, because she is afraid, it is going too fast or not fast enough; because what is she doing here and how did she get here and who is he, this stranger, sitting beside her, naked city toes dancing in the river's edge. She lets her eyes fill with the river. She feels her ears filled with the whoosh of the open water and the shouts of all those workers as they advanced through the streets and over the top of her. Her heart, her recent memory ebbs and flows like dreams, with pain, with awe, with the sound of her breath and the sound of his . . . but at last she speaks. Athene, she says, Athene Brown.

He stands up. He says come with me. His voice is soft, barely loud enough but she hears it, it says come with me. There is a path that meanders beneath the jetties – it is woven from cobbles and sand – and it follows the river's contours and he leads her along it by the hand. She studies the back of him – the dark red circle of his neck, the taut stretch of his shoulders, the fall of his limbs. Sometimes she gasps. She says slow down, wait – but the words blow away down the river, swallowed by the noise and rush of the water and they do not reach him. She says slow down, wait and soon the jetties blend into one and the path becomes a haze and she cannot tell whether she is running or whether he still has hold of her.

She finds herself almost crying. There is a torrent of questions and entreaties and running and please stop and she finds tears on her cheeks, she does not know why but at last he seems to hear her, he stops. He gently brings her hand towards him, turns her round. Now he is laying a cloth on the pebbles. He flicks her up into his arms and he lays her down on the shingle on the foreshore in some far corner of this evening town. He bends over her and he eases the hair back from her face. He runs his index finger over her eyes and her eyebrows, over her nose and her forehead and the rim of her lips. He follows the lines of her cheeks and the edge of her bones. He finds her shoulder again and the length of her arms, he finds her belly-button and the rounds of her knees. He draws images on her, pictures of men and women with their legs entwined and their hearts entwined. He draws them on her face, on her arms, on her waist, pressing her into the folds of him, the warmth of his breath and she has never been here before.

She sings his song. It begins with a smile, it begins with his feel and his touch and the lines that he draws on her stomach. She sings his song, sings it gently as he sings hers, dark against light, rough against smooth. She does not feel the pebbles beneath her back or the cold water that laps around her feet – and the beauty of the chorus runs high, far, long, deep into the chamber of bricks that surrounds them, into the plummeting depths of the river, haunting the empty buildings, buffeting the grasses. And the old man on the corner, heavy brown coat, dirty gnarled boots, he looks up and he knows.

Picture the sun-brown chestnut of her skin, the city-white of his. Picture the slow blink of his eyelids and the gasping stretch of hers. Listen to the air that dances around them – breathless. Listen to the brush of his skin on hers, the soft of his caress, the papery rustle as his shirt grazes against her sea-hard palms. Feel the air as it blows in and out of them, feel the peach touch of her cheek, the long kind blanket of her hair, sit as the young man sits, so close that there is nothing else, no one else … If she does not breathe,

Athene can feel the noise of her beating heart subside. If she centres her weight here, now, on the shingle with the long grasses and the pebbles ribboning through her fingers, Athene can almost feel herself again. Has she forgotten her past? For a moment, it seems possible that she might.

Memory ebbs and flows and years later, Athene struggles to piece it all together. It comes back to her in patches – the words that he says and the words that they share. They sit by the river. She remembers the smells. She remembers the plop-plop as the water gathers around the stays of the bridge and the silent swish as a gull swims by or maybe two.

She remembers him – not his face but him: how at last she feels a presence; how at last solitude is broken and there is a listening heart and someone whose strength she can share. She remembers the heat of him from behind her, just his chest giving off its warmth but it is something she has not known since she was a child when she and Isaiah looked out together over the bright sea.

She remembers standing outside herself at the time – looking down. And there they are no longer sitting side by side but she is lying with her head on his knee and there are long stories – words of all those days alone and all those battles with the seasons. Words of her father, a few; of Dublin Small; of the two Johnnies and how they just left, one day, no warning. Words of this journey here today – of the goodbyes to the sea and the hellos to the city, of the woozy-amber-must, of the rainbow cobwebs and . . .

And she remembers marvelling, it seems a miracle, that she Athene Brown should be sharing the long night; that she should not be afraid; that he is not already preparing to leave.

They take to walking. There is the river, there are the streets that march up and down in grids, there are the huts, there are the sweat-lined alleys that lead to the warehouses, there is the church. They take to sitting and they curl up close and he explains to her all the things, the bridge and all the buildings, the noise, the bustle. She listens to his voice, to the words that draw the maps, lay the bricks, construct the box-shaped windowless buildings that sprawl all around. She hears the rhythm and the logic of the plan, this huge plan which a man and then many men have piled up over the years. She loses herself in its endless threading tapestry but it does not matter, she does not mind, she does not miss the logic of God or the rhythm that God had laid out in Samuel's Bay – because she is with him, resting her head against him, dazed and filled with him.

They visit the warehouse – at night when it is dark, unspeaking. Athene keeps hold of the young man, she is overwhelmed by its labyrinthine size and busyness, by the shuttles and the pots and the bales of cloth that are stacked roof-high in the store-room. She follows him and they step deeper into the building, walk through the corridors of looms. Smell the dye and the dust, the sweat and the effort, hear the echoes of the coughing and the clink of money and the hiss of an egg as it sails through angry air.

They walk the streets – her bare feet, his shoes thip-thip-thapping along night-time roads. March the boundaries of the compound, tiptoeing up to the warehouse owner's front window and giggling when their breath makes patterns on the polished glass. Walk down streets of cabins and streets of shanties that are barely standing and sometimes they wander in and out of the large villas on the top of the hill – climb the garden fences, roll, sniggering, on their lawns. They visit the market where Isaiah used to sell his booty, they visit the church which has an organ, small, reedy, in the corner and wainscoting and some banners that dip down along the aisle and Athene swings her arms round one pillar, reaching her fingers out to be caught by his.

They visit the rotunda that looms roundly in the centre, daisies lined up around its steps like sentries. The young man knows a way in, he has been in here before and he leads her up, round a spiralling staircase. The rotunda smells of polish. Of the old and the new, of the empty and the busy and they follow the staircase which winds up and up. There are doors off it, red doors with no handles, one on each floor but Athene and the young man keep climbing, running their fingers on the cold brass stair-rail, along the grooves that separate the glazed azure tiles.

Eventually, close to the roof, the young man chooses a door, pushes it. They are way up in the gods. Down below, there is light and voices. Athene inches onto the balcony, perches on an old green velvet chair, the young man behind her. She breathes in and the air is metallic. From so far back, Athene cannot distinguish one face from another. There are words but she cannot decipher them and there are bodies, dresses, hats glinting in the light. An elderly woman plays the piano. A man with a stick bangs on the floor and the bodies flutter and Athene has never seen anything like this, fragile, fine, exquisite, and they do not snigger this time but walk back out into the night, united by a precious city secret.

Or they walk beyond the houses, where the town bleeds into the plain and here there is space and quiet. Here among the sward, poppies sway, poppies glow and there is corn or there are reeds, a soft sage velvet, and here she lets her hair out, removes her scarf, roughs up the minute perfection of her skirts or her hats because she knows that here no one can see her. And as her clothes dance atop the hip-high grasses, hats here, gloves there, he draws her down – into the cloud of green, into its sinuous embrace – he draws her down and all you see, from the path, is the dance of the poppies as they nod scarlet in the breeze.

And then they stop walking, on the shingle, in the cushion of the velvet, in the lee of an arch or the shadow of a bridge, and they lie. Sometimes they lie so still for so long that birds walk over them. Sometimes she strokes him, runs her sea-bronzed finger down the side of his face and tries to understand who she is and what she is and how she has come to be here, like this, with him. Her voice a quiet contralto, she hums to him or she whispers to him, tunes from the winds, poems from the lore of the sea. She picks him flowers – wild flowers, flowers that she steals from villa gardens, blooms that droop from trees sick with spring. She draws her finger over his back, pictures of a man and his girl enlaced, and she does not look back, not now.

She forgets the passage of time. Athene Brown sees the town

as a blur, her arrival here as a watery step in a dream. The young man goes away at times – he has meetings, he has rallies – and Athene lies still, listening to the beating of her heart. She tries to picture him, to cut out the line of his face or paint in the colour of his eyes, but he is vague to her, describable only when he is there, in her presence. She tries to reconstruct what it was like before and what it is like now. She thinks back to Samuel's Bay, to the fish, to Isaiah, but the opiate of him – him, him – is in her blood and she rolls over, dazed.

One day the young man takes her with him. Athene sits at the front – the meeting is packed and she has to jostle for space enough to breathe. She listens to his fervour as it whoops in and out of his light frame, as it bounces up and over the heads of all the people who only work there, who only mass together, bond together, comfort in their numbers. The words are no more than murmurs to her, a blend of anger and indignation that she does not understand, but she is proud to be there, at his feet, in the circle of his leader's vision.

Then later she lies, head in his lap, lets him talk about it – about the strikes and the battle; about the warehouse owners and the roof and the weavers and their weary lungs. She hears words like stalemate. She hears words like fruitless and hopeless. She hears how his young-man zeal is fraying, how the price of fervour is costing him dear, how it is hard for them all because they are suffering, they are being paid less and there are one or two, just one or two who shun him, blame him.

And Athene loves him then because there is something he

needs from her, something she can give him. She lets him speak his words and there is no judgment from her. She lets him bewail the passivity of the weavers, the entrenched stubbornness of the mill-owners. She lets him talk of his vision, of the way he will make things better, make things more even, upend the time-honoured system because why should it remain the same, why should it always be that the weavers live pressed together in cabins and the mill-owners luxuriate in grand villas aloof in grand gardens. She is a stranger here and she does not tell him you alone cannot do this. She is a child and a girl and yet she is not daunted by his power or his need for power and she does not say the mill-owners will not change and she does not say and neither will the workers.

She lies head in his lap while the words hum out and she feels the tension in his chest as slowly it eases. She loves him with her hands and her eyes, with her listening heart and her easy detachment. And one day – perhaps it was all just one day – they sit again by the river's edge. There is a stillness between them, a calm. The river roars, the river rushes in front of them. Behind, the town shimmers. Buildings seethe with people, streets writhe under their weight, the warehouse strikers growl their discontent. But between the young man and Athene, there is a calm. They sit and share the pleasure of recent memory. They do not speak but their thoughts are the same. They do not move and they do not touch but they are entwined. The young man smiles – she looks at him and she smiles – and he returns her smile, lifts the curtain of his lips, moves his nose towards hers, presses against her own and there is his breath. He puts his hand, soft-pearl fingers under the drape of her hair and he lifts it gently from her neck. And on this day, more than any other, they love.

Where did they live in those early days? Where did they rest their heads? In truth, it was hard for Athene in years to come to remember. Maybe they skipped between this corner and that corner, between this deep doorway and that. Maybe they dug a hole – hip-deep hole – in the mudflat that lay somewhere close to the outskirts of the town and slept, two fish in a can, two peas in a pod. Or maybe they used the compound, curled up among the bales of silk and slept there, conspiratorial, their night-time fingers brushing on the slubs.

There was no time to worry about the matter of life. No time, no need for the young man and Athene, they had opened the caves of their desires and they had let their fingers run over new skin, felt the soft, raw, touched and explored, loved and laughed and howled and then had just lain and it was all a blur, a rushing heady blur. Sometimes Athene would lift her head from those days and see she was in a meeting again, there were words, there was him, he was talking, they were listening. Sometimes she would wake and the smell of the dust or the dye would startle her, how did she come here, what was she doing here? Sometimes she would wake in the night and wonder about the bay – picture the Lion Rock and the waves, picture her cabin and the boats and the iron-black sand. Then she would feel a nudge, she would look over, there he would be – her man, her boy – and it would all go, all that need to be connected.

And how long did it last? For how many years did they float like thistledown on the wind, did they wander through the city, barefoot, wild, free? Ask Athene and she could never remember for it was too short and the memories slipped through her fingers like water. Ask the young man and he could never tell you for he is dead now. Ask anyone who sat on the streets, who lurked on the corners, ask the old man, heavy brown coat, dirty gnarled boots – and they would not know. Maybe a year, maybe ten. Maybe a day, maybe an hour. They ran and they floated; they loved and they floated; they laughed and they ate and he spoke and she listened and they floated.

Three

There was youth. There was innocence and levity. There were times when touch was like pain and words were like drops of magic water. There was the swoon of love, the rushing downhill hurtle of love, the times when they could not stop and they could not listen because their hearts were filled and their days were filled.

And then all in a day, everything changes. Athene Brown wakes up and she knows she is carrying a child. The young man wakes up and discovers his protest has crumbled, the workers can take it no longer, they have capitulated. Athene Brown walks the streets and in the distance, she is sure she sees old Ivy Peacock. The young man walks the streets and a sharp stone hits him on the side of the head.

All in a day, everything changes. Athene Brown looks in her shell-encrusted mirror and sees fuller lips and brighter eyes. She sees lustrous hair and thick lashes and she feels her breasts, they are woman-breasts and she knows she is carrying a child. Athene Brown looks down at the young man but for now it is her secret. She leaves him there, sleeping.

She goes for a walk because now there is focus. Now there is a need to concentrate and she wants to think about it all, think about what lies ahead and what there has been that has brought her here. She wanders through the patchwork of the city, skirting through its layers, only she does not pay attention to that because there is too much to consider inside. The grand villas look on and the rotunda in the square looks on and the church and the bridges and the warehouses look on while Athene Brown contemplates this change in her situation. Is she delighted? Is this a token of her love for the young man? Will she be a radiant, joyful mother – growing in strength as she watches her child grow in its turn? Is this a bond, gift from God, and it will unite them, unite their fates, bringing two lives into one?

Athene Brown runs her hand over her still-flat stomach. She crosses her arms and secretly cups each breast with each hand – as she walks now by the river, as her eyes catch the glide of the barges, moving under the inscrutable gaze of the old men. She goes to sit down now – on that creel. Time is going fast. She has had barely a few months to adjust to the town, no time to reflect on the bay, to pull back, stand outside this passion she shares with the young man – and now she is expecting a child. Athene scuffs her feet on the dirt of the river bank. She wipes her forehead because today is hot, there is no air. She runs the tip of her finger over the sequins on her scarf, they are covered in dust, it is something to distract her from her thoughts. Athene looks up and across the river, she catches a glimpse of some woman, she is sure it is Ivy Peacock.

*   *   *

She lays it aside – when she finds him again and she is bold enough to tell him, she lays aside the fact that she has seen one of the old people here. She goes to tell him instead about the child, about the fact that soon they will share more than snatched moments. She realises as she pours it all out that her heart is lifting, she is going to be a mother! She says it all in a rush. She says it all where up until now it has mostly been him. She realises as she speaks that they have rarely spoken of themselves, that they know little of what each has experienced and she sees it all, stretching out before them, a lifetime of words and joy and stories and her heart fills some more because now, there is so much to say.

She is so filled with this – a new love – that she does not wait for him. She does not watch his face. She does not watch the words as they wing their way towards him, how there is a crucial pause before they seem to be taken in. She does not see the crushed look in his eyes, the hint of something wounded, only now it is more than a hint. She does not notice how his shoulders are drooping and he has lost his sheen, something terrible has happened . . .

Years later, when she looks back on that moment, Athene Brown asks herself if perhaps this was all too soon for him. Perhaps then he was still in part just a boy, not ready to be a father or a husband, only a lover and an adventurer, a warrior. Perhaps she could see that he only really loved her in so far as she held up a mirror to him. How could they unite when they came from such different lives? How could they love and be together and stay together when, in some small way, they were both so alike – both leaders, fighters, loners?

Athene Brown waits for his reaction. She waits for him to stand up, eyes gleaming. The dippers who are there beside them, on the shingle, pecking through the sand for grubs, they wait too. The old men on their barrels, they know once again something intriguing is happening and they turn to watch, wait for the air to ring out with a whoop of yippee, wait for his face to fold in a smile of joy. Athene stands up. She needs him to draw her up because to sit down and kiss is not enough, it does not show enough how suddenly they are filled with pride, with hope, with triumph. She needs him to wrap his birdoflove in the tight knit of his arms, to let the dippers see as tawny-brown girl, city-white boy embrace – on the verge of the deep-dark river – in love, in the selfish parcel of love.

She wants to tell everyone. She wants everyone to know, to be filled with happiness because she is. She stops people who are walking over the bridge, she tells men with barrows and men on boats and the butcher and the churchwarden and the old man, heavy brown coat, dirty gnarled boots, who sits on the corner. She runs up the church steps, she runs in and out of the bazaar, she runs down on the shingle and in and out of the stays that tiptoe lightly in the waters. She sings, Athene sings and her voice rings through the town. She smiles and the gleam of it flashes out, across the river, in and out of the warehouse windows. She holds his hand – she will not let go – enlacing her fingers with his so that now they are one not once but twice and the people who see them and the people whom she tells, they too are happy because how could you not be happy to see a pair so wild barefoot free.

For most of that day, Athene Brown is filled with a rapt whoop of pleasure – she is going to be a mother, mother of his child, joined for ever with him . . .

But the selfish parcel of love is quickly unwrapped and earlier in the day the workers retired in groups to discuss the situation that has developed since the Big Day. Since then, there has been no work. Since then, the warehouse has been shut and the skeins of silk have sat gathering dust like the bottles of dye and the looms. The ladies in the villas have gone without fabric but, worse, the weavers and their families, they have suffered, they have gone without food and the principles of the fight – the dustfromtheroof and the wewantmorepay – have become lost in a daily grind of hunger and idle hands.

At first the young man was their leader. He took the essence of their struggle and he enshrined it in words that the weavers could never have thought of. He took the plight of those who coughed and the avariciousness of those who counted the coins plink-plink and he weighed them up, one against the other – and it seemed right, what he did, Absolutely Right. He took the story of each roof fibre and he spelt them out, shouts of righteous indignation, and he made the mill-owners tremble with his threats of no work and nothing-to-sell. If there were doubters, his fierce zeal won them round. If there were those who wished to hide, he showed them that in the end, they would come to regret their own timidity.

But the young man and the weavers did not understand

that at that point, the cycle of history was against them. The order of things was not ready to crumble, the mill-owners were not ready to relinquish their villas on the hill, the weavers were not ready to accept the rigorous caveats that would accompany a higher wage.

They have used the young man and today the weavers decide they will use him again – they will hold him up as a scapegoat to the mill-owners. They will go to the mill-owners and say it was not our idea. They will let it be known – throughout all the other warehouses, all the other places where unrest has been rife – that all along, it was the young man. All along, it was his idea to strike, it was his idea to fight for more pay, better conditions. After all, they say – on this day, the day when Athene Brown dances on a cloud of happiness – he is only young. After all, they say, we did not truly believe all he said. And in any case, they add, what other choice do we have?

Athene Brown has put to the back of her mind her sighting of Ivy Peacock. She has run her hand over her new woman-breasts, looked into her bright full-woman eyes. She has sung and danced her way through the town, she has smiled out, she has winked at the old man on the corner – and all the while, the weavers have been plotting the downfall of her lover.

Athene Brown knows nothing of their plots, just as she knew little of the strikes as they progressed. She does not know – nor will she ever – just how bitterly let down the young man feels when he hears of their capitulation. She has no inkling of the darkness that has swamped him, this very morning – because as a member of a family of silk-weavers, he too has always suffered; because he too has always had to live in squalor, listening to his mother cough her way to oblivion, watching his father grow weaker, more listless by the day. Athene Brown attributes then the young man's passive, careless response to the news of their child – as she will attribute it always – to wider causes, to immaturity, to the unfathomable differences between the sexes, to shock. She believes she knows the young man's story – but she knows nothing of its roots.

The day is coming to an end and Athene Brown wishes to dispel the grain of doubt that lurks in her mind about him. She wishes to take him to the river bank, to sit beside him on the shingle, to face him, ask him, talk to him, listen to him; to cajole him, woo him, love him and know that none of this will ever have been in vain. She wishes to take his hand and place it on her belly. She wishes to take his fingers and bring them to her lips. She wants to exact from him a promise that he will never leave her – she feels so confident in his love, she can ask him this – as all the others did.

The day is coming to an end and Athene Brown walks with the young man towards the foreshore. It has been so hot today, humid. The wind that whips the sea, that makes the iron-black sand puff in circles, it does not reach the town, not often, so damp air lingers, suet-heavy. Now, that heat is infused with dusk. Athene Brown listens to the soft pad of their footsteps. She watches a small bead of sweat as it trickles down his temple. She listens to the beating of her heart and she is sure she can hear another, beating alongside.

*   *   *

When the stone wheels through the air, it is meant as an emblem of frustration. It is meant to show the young man how very tired they all are, how worn out with the worry, how disappointed that his efforts and theirs have been to no avail. The stone is thrown by a child – a girl. She has dirty-dark eyes and long brown-black hair. She does not work in the warehouse but both her mother and her father do, while she – she stays at home. She cooks the food. She makes the little ones eat and the little ones go to sleep. The girl has no name nor will she ever. The girl is only a messenger, like the stone, an emblem. She does not mean to hurt the young man. She does not mean the stone to hit him on the side of the head, to knock him out cold, to cause sufficient damage to his brain then and there that it is apparent, even to Athene who knows little of medicine, that the young man will never live to see his child.

The stone wheels through the air because the young man is used as a scapegoat. The weavers wish him to carry the brunt of the blame for the failure of the strikes, because it would be too heavy, too uncomfortable for them. The gods wish him to carry the brunt of the blame because, in years to come, when conditions in the warehouse deteriorate still further, the young man himself will become an emblem. His death will become a notch in history, leading ultimately to better days for the weavers, then to mechanisation, then to wholesale redundancy.

Athene Brown has no such wish. She runs her hand along his cheek as he lies motionless on the dirt-dust road. She pulls off her sequin-embroidered scarf and she tucks it under his head, then wraps the tail over the open wound.

She takes her fist, slender but clenched tight-tight and she rams it into her mouth. Tears fall from her woman-bright eyes. Down onto her still-flat woman-filling belly.

Four

W hen Athene Brown was nigh on seventy, she sent her daughter a gift. It was a stickleback. The stickleback was carved from tortoiseshell, its complex architecture of fins complete in every detail. The stickleback was tiny – it filled the cup of Iris's palm, no more. It was thin, almost thin as paper, so much so it almost curled in the warmth of her hand and you could tell from its delicate fragile nature that it was the product of years of work. Iris held the fish gently between thumb and forefinger, turned it round in the light. She saw the precious dappling of the fabric itself and then the intricate, painstaking incisions made by the point of a knife or the edge of its blade. Deep inside the mouth of the fish – which was agape – Iris thought she could see two letters and a date. Time and again, she tried to make out what they said. She was sure they were initials – were they those of her father?

For sure he was a mystery – but Athene Brown carries his growing seed inside her and she vows to herself, to the memory of those she has lost, to the mill-workers who toil hard, no air to breathe, that she will allow this seed to grow. She wants to lie down and let the wash of pain subsume her – but she will not, cannot. She wants to breathe out one last time and never let another speck of dust, grain of sand, whiff of salt, spray of water cross her lips or travel around her system – but she will not, cannot. Grief – like a thick, thick blanket – envelops her. Pain, so sharp she is almost afraid to breathe, pumps inside her chest. Here at her feet is her saviour. Here, with his head split open and his blood pulsing out onto the street, is someone who saw in her something she did not know she had. Athene Brown looks up and around – to see the source of the stone? To see a little girl, dirty-dark eyes as she turns, runs away, back into the shadows from which she came? To shout out This IsNotRight, ThisShouldNotBeDone? To stare back at the onlookers, to stare through her blurred vision, stare then hiss then fold like a crumpled leaf ?

With the tip of her finger, she runs over the features of his face. Takes her fingers to his lips. Takes his hand, limp, places it gently softly on her belly. Feels the response of an unfamiliar pulse and she vows I will let this seed grow.

As she did with Dublin Small all those years before, Athene Brown picks up the young man. Like Dublin Small, the young man is not heavy – he was strong, it was true, but the fire burnt so bright inside, there was precious little room for flesh. The last drop of life has seeped away and Athene Brown carries the young man like an armful of flowers. She feels a small pull of the muscles in her stomach but she pays no attention, only she heads slowly to the silk compound.

Early evening streets bow down to watch her go. Watch her cloche hat as it perches on her sun-reddened hair. Watch her heavy steps, watch the tiny pockets of light as they glint off her scarf.

The warehouse gate creaks on its axis. There is no one here but there has been someone here today, she can tell, the air is cleaner, the looms seem poised for action. She lays him down on a table. Chance would have it be the same table he laid her on those tumultuous months back – but Athene has no care for chance. She does not look up again at the rainbow cobwebs. She does not marvel again at the bales of cloth or the skeins of silk. She lays him down on the table and she pulls the door to and she hears the gate again, as it grumbles shut behind her.

Death and life, night and day travel hand in hand – and Athene Brown does not know where to go, what to do. Now it is night, death, and once again she is alone. Once again the spectre of her past looms large. She unpacks her bag and Isaiah, Samuel's Bay, Samuel himself, the fish-storm, Dublin Small, the Carnival of the Fish, the young man all lie arrayed before her. Her mother Comfort too and Ezekiel and all the fishermen who were there first and all the townsmen who preceded them. All the weavers and all the mill-owners, all the men who built the cabins and the church, all the women with their washing bottoms, all their children, lying out in rows. Destiny beckons her but Athene Brown is too shaken to read the signal. There is only one direction she can take – because of who she is, because of the accident of her experience and the culmination of all the seeds implanted in her by all who have gone before.

But Athene Brown hesitates – after all, time has been flowing fast.

She finds herself walking. Out of the town, away from the cabins that feather into the plain. Out of the view of the villas and the church, away from the cool dark river. Watched as she leaves by the children from the young man's house, by the girl who threw the stone dirty-dark eyes, by Ivy Peacock who cluck-clucks through her reedy teeth well fancy that.

No map, no plan but she describes as she later sees it a huge crescent. She walks up-country, not on the coast but following the contours of the island all the same. Bag full of ghosts on her shoulder, small growing seed bumping up and down inside her belly. She hears hello from the men who are tending their cattle in the fields, hello from farmers and workers, from a gravedigger here, some road-builders there. Sometimes she works, she helps with the harvest, she sweeps out a barn. She takes food that is offered, shelter – but she shares nothing, not her thoughts, not the tumult that whirls inside, not the dread-cum-fear-cum-excitement that surely she feels at the forthcoming birth of her child.

She goes deeper, inside the country. There is a rising mountain, volcanic, snow or is it a cloud perched at the top. Here it is verdant, blue to purple the higher you go. The sun is here as it always was at Samuel's Bay but here it is only illumination for you climb the mountain and you grow cold to your bones. Athene comes down the mountain, finds herself in a forest. The forest is rich, primary, filled with birds and it opens out into a valley and the valley puffs out steam, hot yellow froth bubbling up from inside. From the geysers to the valleys, from the mountains to the plain, Athene walks and the rhythm of her steps matches the rhythm of her broken heart. She lets the months of the town and the months, years of her struggle in the bay be pushed out by new panoramas, by new sights, smells, new hope.

Sometimes during that longest of journeys, when Athene travels but she has nowhere to go, when she wanders her land but she has little interest in what she sees, Athene pauses – not only to work but maybe to rest awhile. Soon her past and her future are going to collide, soon she is going to be mother to a child – a girl, she is sure of that. Athene Brown wants to hold it off. She wants to keep the collision back because she is not ready yet, she is bruised and damaged by events far beyond her control but events which she feels all the same she must have brought upon herself.

To hold it off, she hones in on the little things. She pulls out her bag and she empties it out. She takes her cloche hat, felt and she cuts off the beads that were woven in patterns of the sea and she threads them into one tiny bracelet and one tiny necklace. She cuts up layers of an organdie dress and makes them into sheets and a cover for a basket and she takes the basket she stole from the market and she decks it out so that it looks ready for a princess and she makes a cup, a tiny sipping cup from the rest of the turtle shell she found all those years ago on the beach at Samuel's Bay.

Sometimes, as she works, she wonders about the young man. She runs her mind over his agile driven body. She listens to his voice and she hears his big words and his passion. She wonders what would have happened if that stone had not been thrown, would it have worked, would they have continued to share dreams, loving, where would they be. Would they have sat one day on their veranda's edge, old woman, old man, watched their child, their child's children, while all those years of complicity ensured their hands, their hearts, their thoughts remained enlaced?

Fate had made her impassive to its vicissitudes. Fate had made her strong, aloof and she had pulled inside herself and then the young man came, he gave her a glimpse of a girl who could live outside, who could love, who need not be fearful . . .

Athene's journey which has described the island begins to return in on itself. She is close to having her child so her progress is slow. Athene skirts round villages and towns. She works on farms, she takes refuge in farms, she walks again – unable to stop for long for then she is obliged to follow the train of her thoughts. She feels her child grow inside. She feels tiny hands press against her belly, tiny feet. She watches her dress as it takes on a life of its own, as it billows outwards, forwards without her.

At last she reaches the coast, west coast. Here the sea has plenty to digest – thick walls of rock, long stretching dunes of sand, earth yielding as sugar. The sea works hard. Athene skirts the crags and at times she is misted by spray. She moves inland, the topography obliges her to do so and yet there is no escaping it, the smell, the sound, the all-pervading power of the sea – chasing her, haunting her, beckoning her.

Were she not so ground-heavy, Athene Brown might feel something – pang of nostalgia perhaps. Scent of the sea, feel of the salt, sound of the roar and the crash and the blue. Red of the wind, green of the sky and she might almost be back again, home again. She might almost have returned to Samuel's Bay, back where her story began, all those million immemorial years before . . .

Part Four

One

Picture Isaiah as he sits today on the deck of his red boat. Anchor down, home again at last, sun on his face, sea flat-calm. The air is gritty, salty, filled with sound. Gulls wheel overhead, their plaintive oboe cry never coming to an end while the waters slap – slap-slap – against the gnashing teeth of the Deadmen. Beneath the long shadow of the Lion Rock, Isaiah seems small today, frail. His lungs have become severely debilitated and it is a struggle to breathe, a struggle to reach from one moment to the next. Isaiah does all he can to sit still, no motion at all. He tries to hold himself, no panic, let the air come slowly – burrowing deep down inside so his heart, his chest can cease crying with pain. And then, with droplets of peace hard won in this growing battle between life and death, Isaiah can delve back into the hiddenmost pockets of his past.

When Isaiah was a child, the single most vivid occasion he witnessed was the Carnival of the Fish. Once every seven years – since the advent of Samuel, since the paradise of the bay had been discovered by the townsfolk – they had held a carnival. Samuel started it himself, he celebrated it on his own with a boat or two, with a fish or two, with a flag that he had made from old cloths washed up on the shore. And then Samuel died and the townsfolk came and they knew of his one-man carnival and they perpetuated the tradition because this, it seemed to them, embodied the essence of their existence.

Isaiah sits in his boat at the mouth of Samuel's Bay and he is back at his first carnival. He sees black of the sand and white of the cloud. He sees red of the wind and green of the seas beyond. The rows of coloured huts glint in the sand like gems spilt from a basket – blood-red and grass-green, corn-yellow and deep-sea blue. Rusting tin roofs shimmer in the sun, tipping tin chimney stacks beckon like crooked fingers – and there atop the roaring, soaring Lion, he sees a seven-year-old child, small-boy hand encased in that of his father.

Isaiah sees himself with Ezekiel and they are looking down – on the men, women, children, on the noise and the hubbub, on the feasting and the dancing, when the fishermen laugh, when they sing, when they drink and it does not matter if the wind blows the sands or the rain smears their painted faces because today is the Carnival of the Fish and God knows they may never hold another. Boats are nodding on the waters. Flags festoon the Lion and they run from his nose to his paws, from his tail across the beach to the rows of multi-coloured cottages behind. Strips of white cloth flutter from the cutty-grass and there are garlands on the flax bushes and etched into the rocky façade at the far end of the beach there is a huge profile of a fish drawn with white chalk, embroidered with leaves of the trees that surround the bay and leaves from the flowers that lean out in heavy bunches between the dunes. There are tables out, littering the iron-black sand. There are gongs and drums, there are chairs and buckets of fruit, there are people and they are scrubbed into cleanness and spryness and they shine with expectation.

Isaiah is just seven and he watches rapt as men wrestle on the beach. He sees a great circle etched in the sand. It is flagged and two men dance in and out of each other's grasp within the circle. Gongs chime. Drums roll. The men tussle in the dust. All day long, beneath the gaze of the chalky fish, in the shadow of the Lion, the competition runs. There are knock-out rounds and though there are not many contenders, it can take from first light until dusk for the title to be decided – the winner the man who defeats all the others, the man whose strength, endurance, prowess remain unchallenged.

Out on the sea, another contest takes place. Contest between man and fish. Contest between the young pretenders of the bay and the mighty warriors of the deep. Competitors have rowed out in their boats. On deck they have rods, spears, nets, lines. Isaiah sees how their backs glint in the sun, shiny with oil. He sees how they trawl the sea, far out, searching for the marlin – the fighter. He remembers watching that year, how it was a young Ron Cuckelty who had the luck, how his little boat was towed up and down, how the fish thrashed and you saw its tail; how the man flailed and the lines tugged and you saw the long spear of its snout or the sharp ridges of its fins; how once or twice, it leapt clean from the water –

huge, angry, snaking, all-powerful – and there was a vision of colour, flashes of blue, yellow, black glancing off its sides. How the fight lasted all day, how Ron came and went, how the battle ebbed and flowed – and then it was dead, spear jutting out of its side, sand sticking to its scales, colour and power, majesty fading in the heartless gaze of the sun.

Isaiah sits on the sky-warm deck of his boat, reliving that day. He hears the shouting and the go-ons. He hears the get-hims and the look-outs. He hears the soft thuds as the men hit the sand and he hears the shrieks of the women and the fluttering of the bunting and the rustle of the flax bushes and below it all, the low-tone music of the drums. Isaiah sits here today, old man now, feels himself tug on his father's fingers. He feels his feet itching to slither down the Rock, to run across the sand. He feels himself yearning, his heart yearning to take part in the wrestling young though he is, to fight gleaming muscles sweating chests, to throw them over, earn his part in the history of the bay. He feels the disappointment again when he is obliged to remain up there, to look down only, when his father will not let him go. He feels the closeness again that his father imposed upon him and mostly it was a bond, it was something magnifying, but in part it was a girdle, cast-iron corset, and it did not allow the young Isaiah to breathe.

Since he left the town, Isaiah has thought many times of all those chances – to win a fight, to fight a fish, to become part of the weft of legend. He has thought of Ezekiel and their days as man and boy. Of the times when they gathered the logs, gathered the kindling, built a fire; of the times when the man worked a tool and the boy looked on; of the times when they shared the pleasure of grilled fish, fresh fruit, elderberry wine and the boy might say something, he might make a shy comment – about the wind, about the sea, about another child from the village – and the man would smile or the man would rebuke or the man would tap his pipe on the floor, look thoughtful.

He has thought of Comfort, of how it might have been had she not died – how they might have lived together, fought and struggled and loved together, how they might have talked, sat together of an evening in the glinting, treasure-filled cabin she would call home, listened to the sea-chimes ringing, then and always, with the sound of the sea.

But for all the slow old-age pleasure of nostalgia, Isaiah has dreaded to return to the subject of his daughter. It is as though some guilt has evolved, the closer he has come to returning home.

For sure, Isaiah makes his return as slow as he can. How long might it take him – to go from the frenzy of the town through the flat plain of the sea, to sail from the boatyard to the bay? Isaiah could do it in a day. One evening he could sail out of the boatyard – the next he could be sailing home, into the arms of those craggy rocks he has known since he was a boy.

And he could picture it all. He could see his journey's end – he would come to the bay and he would find her grave; or he would come here and he would find the place empty, there would be no one, only abandoned huts and scraps of old boats and no fish and no fishermen. He would relive the fish-storm and follow in his mind the logic of the consequences of all that wind, all that destruction – and there it would be, in front of him, evidence of all that he had lived by these past years, evidence of his daughter's death and all their deaths, evidence of the demise of the bay.

But Isaiah leaps into his hard-won, town-built boat and though he means to go back, he finds it is too soon. Were he only braver, he might explain to himself the truth of his fear. He might admit to himself that the girl he saw in the town that day looked so uncannily like Comfort before her, how could it be anyone else but Athene? There were his wintergreen eyes; there was sea-bronzed skin and sea-weathered hair; the trail of a voice, so like Ezekiel's in timbre – that laugh, that smile, that taste for clothes that glitter, shimmer . . . if Isaiah were braver, he could say perhaps I was mistaken. If he were stronger, he could be overjoyed – she is alive! If he were more generous, he could go up to the young man (for he has seen them together) – clap him hard on the back and he could wrap the girl tight in his arms and he could act, make things better . . .

Isaiah's unacknowledged fear is matched only by his panic, his uncertainty. It was just a glimpse – it was just a whiff. Could it be her? Why would she be here and how could she have survived and why did he never know? Isaiah runs through in his mind all the possibilities that could have led to his being reunited before now with Athene. Perhaps some of the old people could have come to the town to look for him. Perhaps they could have seen him – at the market, in the street, by the river and they could have said why Isaiah, you're alive. They could have said and did you know, by the way, so is your girl. Uncertainty leads Isaiah to doubt himself. To doubt what he saw, to doubt the force of his instinct. And panic leads him to muddle it all up, to forget that he thought they all had died. To forget also that he too was supposed to have died. To confuse the pattern of events and the pattern of possibilities so much in his mind that by turns he is sure it was her and convinced it could not be.

Perhaps now after twenty years in the city Isaiah is old enough, mature enough to understand just what happened to him when he became separated from his past. Perhaps now Isaiah can understand that in some way, all this time skirting through the layers of the town has been a form of grieving. He has hidden from his past because it was too painful, too riven with tragic loss.

But if Isaiah is ready to understand that, he is not ready to understand that what he did – when he dived from the Lion, when he swam through the sea, when he came to in the town and he chose not to return, not at any point throughout those previous twenty years – was to abandon his daughter.

So he disappears into the flat plain of the sea and he is afraid of what he must do next. He needs to return to Samuel's Bay and yet to do so seems fraught with risk. What will he say to himself, what will he say to the gods and the winds if he understands from going there that he surely did, he surely left her? How will he dare to go on living, to face himself, to confront such cowardice if that was the case?

How will he dare to offer his own life to the sea again if he knows that he – a man capable of love, a man born of love – chose wilfully to walk away from one of his own?

Each time his thoughts return to the possibility that Athene might have survived the storm, Isaiah gets up. He moves about, he clears his throat, he coughs – long, deep *hhwerrgh* which seems uninclined to stop at the bottom of his lungs. He plays with his sail, his oars. He sweeps the deck, he tidies it. Excessive movement makes his heart thud. It makes his lungs splutter and his ribs heave further and in some ways this helps Isaiah, it distracts him from having to think any further about anything but regaining his equilibrium.

There are men, afraid of death, who bring about their own destruction. Fearful of mortality, they hurtle towards it, anxious to tackle it before it tackles them. Isaiah is no such man. Isaiah leaves the town and he turns left. He heads north, away from Samuel's Bay. He allows himself to think it was a fluke of the winds. He says it was a mistake, my mistake, never mind, I can always turn round. The town disappears behind him – the huts and the workers, the old boys on their barrels. Isaiah knows nothing of the collapse of the strike but when the sunset is swallowed by darkness, he lights a lantern, sits back, watches it bob up and down on the breeze.

Years later, as she read through his spidery watercolour sketchings of that journey and all his journeys, Isaiah's granddaughter tried to plot the passage that he followed on his tiny red boat. She tried to picture all he saw, all those years before – her island from the sea, when the coastline remained as yet unsullied by the reckless hand of Progress.

Isaiah sees from the sea what Athene has only skirted around from the land. Rock-hugging villages – tight clusters of cottages, multi-coloured, hanging on to the lip of the land. Roaring rising plinths of dark basalt, shaped as men or as monsters, sharp as axes; inlets black and silver, waters turning from amethyst to amber as the sun rises and falls. There are caves, mouths open, wanting to swallow him. There are long stretches of sand when you see no one and you hear no one and you are utterly alone. There are marshy expanses and all you hear is the cry of a wader, long, sad, reaching out inland, seawards, and you do not know how to answer. There are strings of islands, jewels of iridescent green, and Isaiah wonders if every one has been explored. There is a long peninsula, it seems like a sleeping giant and Isaiah navigates round this, noticing the flora as he goes, noticing the thick canopy of hardwoods, the softer umbrella of ferns beneath.

At first Isaiah travels and he absorbs himself in the detail of his journey. There is the boat to handle, there is the weather to gauge. There are storms to avoid, there are rocks to avoid, there is a host of unfriendly minutiae which he can use to postpone the true object of his thoughts. There are contours to follow – for somehow Isaiah is reluctant to sail away from here altogether – and there is the constant lurking surprise of unforeseen menace. Perhaps a bull-nosed shark; or a series of rocks skulking just beneath the waterline; perhaps whirling eddies in the

179

currents which you do not see until it is almost too late; perhaps ropes fraying and then there is a journey to find new ropes or new flax or something, some way of holding up the sails. One day Isaiah's mast snaps – as though one of the gods just reached down and bent it in two between his fingers – and Isaiah has to limp into the shore, hunt out the right materials. One day Isaiah finds a hole in the side of his boat and it is a mystery how it came or when but again Isaiah is obliged to go ashore, to work with his saw and his plane, make things right.

Isaiah journeys and he becomes absorbed in its nuts and bolts. But slowly something else happens, something he had not nor could ever have anticipated. Isaiah finds he is a natural voyager. He finds pleasure, sharp fierce pleasure in all that he sees – in all that changes and all that remains the same. He looks up and there is an albatross hanging high, high in the wind. He looks inland and he sees a pair of grebes involved in some exotic ritual dance, heads like cobras', dancing on the verge of a volcanic pool. He breathes in – when he has the strength – and smells salty-soot of the sea; or fresh white of the wind; or the rich tang of nectar, a hibiscus is in flower on the sand.

Time assumes a quality he cannot grasp. Time, space, movement, shape dissolve. Isaiah finds he enters a voyage of the imagination where there are no looms and no strikes; where the beauty of the work of the gods surpasses everything; where rhythm and balance – the rhythm of the planet, the balance of nature – pulse in his blood and he rows on the sea or he moors and walks on the land and everything, everything else seems minor by comparison.

He weathers storms. He weathers droughts and deluges, acute hunger. He fights the elements, his health suffering but somehow he is not deterred – as though Isaiah himself has become part of the journey. He feels the extremes of solitude as he has never felt them before – travelling through other lives, sailing through waters he will never know, moving or stopping but never staying. Only once he pushes out to the open ocean. He loses sight of the land and almost all bearing. The wind has died down and all there is is the sound of his beating heart; that and the soft plip-plip-plip of a shoal of flying fish as they thread in a silver hoop-la into the waves a few yards from his prow.

And as this peace seems slowly to descend on Isaiah and as he sees too that there is not much time left to him, so he begins to record an account of his time at Samuel's Bay and his time in the town. Slowly – because he is no historian; painfully because words are not Isaiah's currency. He puts it down thinking that he can relive it all as he goes. He traces the story from the beginning of the bay to his own return, when it comes.

Isaiah finds immense relief as he does so. He is able to explain to himself the pattern of his life; to understand the foibles of those who made him and to grasp at least in part his own peculiarities; to relive his love for his father but also to understand his father as a human being, to see that he was someone as robustly and heartbreakingly fallible as any man; to relive his love for Comfort, to see that that was the point at which fate was really cruel, the moment when she died in childbirth.

Isaiah does not work every day on his project. Indeed initially he does not see this work as a project, simply as a natural extension of his journey. He allows himself to dwell in the moments left to him. He prefers to go to his thoughts lovingly. He likes to savour the way they ooze thick slow onto his paper. He finds too that he wishes to be honest, to see the thing from all sides and sometimes this does not come easily for there are parts of his story where honesty has often been avoided.

But gradually it comes – a jigsaw of remembrance; a patchwork of his thoughts and his father's deeds, of Samuel's heroism and the vicissitudes of a life working with nature; a collage of his days with Comfort, his days on the sea; around the edges, memories of the others – Dublin Small, the two Johnnies, the women with their washing bottoms, the children. He etches in the struggle to survive. He describes it and he rues it and although he is not capable of offering any answer, he hopes that this description alone will make the matter seem a little closer to being tackled.

As he goes, Isaiah colours it also – choosing tints he can make from materials of the sea. Ground-up shells or sand and he does it in watercolour, minute pointillist pictures of all that he sees and all that he has known. Dot-dot-dot for a boat, dot-spot-swish and there is his father, clear to Isaiah as day, alive on the page. Dot-block-splodge and he is back in his early days in the town; swish-swish-smudge and he is there in the hazy atmosphere of the silk factory. Each page is roughly but lovingly hewn from the deep well of his past. Sometimes there is only one word to a page, with one image – perhaps that of a stickleback or a minke whale, perhaps that of the Lion Rock, soaring in all his splendour out of a molten amber sea.

The progress of the work matches Isaiah's progress around his island. Now Isaiah finds he no longer fears his return to Samuel's Bay. Now that he is coming to understand his destination, Isaiah can savour the journey. He has reached the tip of the island and now he descends the western seaboard. Here the coast is altogether craggier for here the sea is angry, whipped up by the winds he remembers from his childhood. Isaiah passes fjords. He passes coves hiding from the wind and a lighthouse or two and rocks not of basalt but granite – uncompromising and sheer.

Isaiah sails gently as the winds allow him. He takes his time, stopping when he can or he has to, moving on as he chooses. He works in his cabin or he works on deck. You hear him, head bent low as he murmurs the ideas to himself. You see him, curled up inside himself, drawing it out. Every now and again, the peaceability of his work is disturbed by the dreadful legacy of the warehouse, by huge lung-trawling coughs that threaten to suffocate him then and there. But between times, he presses on. Not urgently, only slowly.

Two

When Athene was eight or nine and she was being looked after by Dublin Small and the two Johnnies, there was a favourite game that they played when the wind died down. It meant climbing up to the clearing in the cutty-grass and listening, closely, minutely to every sound. From up there, you had an unusually limpid aural picture of the bay. Dublin and the two Johnnies would take their time to get there but Athene used to spring up the hill and crouch in the clearing shouting Beat you! When at last they caught her up, they would all three be wheezing, Dublin cursing his limbs and his lungs and every blessed part of him.

In actual fact it was Dublin who was most skilled at the game. Years of sitting on a chair in the sand, years of passive observation had taught him the way. The real trick, he showed Athene, was to learn to overlook the sounds in your own body – to block out from your mind the rushing of your blood and the beating of your heart, to reduce yourself to a waiting silent husk. Then said Dublin you will hear plenty – you will even hear the bees as they pollinate the flowers.

These are among Athene's happiest memories of those times – all four silhouetted against the hill, crouching down, holding their breath; all four contained tight within themselves, each following his own path to his own revelation of the secrets that the gods had arrayed all around.

On her return to Samuel's Bay, Athene plans to play this game once again. She means to go up there, to the clearing in the cutty-grass on a day when the wind is not too fierce. She means to crouch down and let them come to her – the sounds of the sea, whisper of a light breeze, perhaps even the snaking of fins, rustle of water, slap-slap of the currents around the Deadmen.

Ask Athene Brown – at any point up until Iris is born – what her expectations of motherhood are and Athene would be unable to answer. How will it be, Athene, how will you feel? For sure, she might say, there is a low incandescent excitement – echo perhaps of that exultation she savoured only too briefly on the day she found out she was pregnant. She is hot too, always hot – furnace of the baby inside keeping her at boiling point – and sometimes Athene might attribute this to expectant pleasure.

But if she genuinely rejoices in her future as a mother to the child she knows will be a girl, Athene Brown does not know it. Sometimes indeed, as she waits for the birth, as she wanders in and out of dreams and the blurred borders between day and night, she curses her state, Isaiah-you-bastard Ezekiel-you-bastard young-man-you-bastard ringing round the tops of the coves, floating down and out to sea with all those gulls and all those waves – as if by blaspheming against her own genesis, against all the other births, she can resist the next.

At others, if she lies down, places her hand on her belly, if she remains still, she can feel her daughter's head. She can trace the outline of her face, the minute snub of a nose. She can feel a butterfly tumble in her belly and it is the kick of feet or the push of fists. If she sits and lets time rest in the palm of her hand, she can hear the clear rhythm of that second heart, tick-tock-tick-tock, beating faster than her own as if that is the only way it can lay claim to life. Athene might revel in these moments but still she is unsure how they will progress.

Even hours later – when Athene is finally released from all that physical urgency, when the wheels of pain have turned and turned and then miraculously come to rest, when she has realised her seminal ill-comprehended need to go home, and now she is here, kitten-mewling soft-wriggling packet of brown-skinned, black-haired flesh-and-cartilage on her chest, muslin billowing in on her cabin windows – Athene would be hard pressed to tell you where she is heading or what she awaits from all of this. There was death and now there is life and it is as though the largeness of the issues has been forced into retreat.

All her plans – even the smallest one, to play the listening game, even the grandest plan, to resume the mission of the fish – are put into abeyance once Iris is born. Anything that Athene may have anticipated from this is pushed from her mind. All there is is sensation – from one moment to the next, from one landscape to another.

*   *   *

187

Athene looks back years later on those days, early moments of motherhood. There is exhaustion, there is lingering pain, there is the discomfort of an ageing cabin, ageing bed, not much to make a home from – but also, there are for moments completeness, an absolute self-sufficiency that Athene has forgotten could possibly exist. Hot sea-wind and she sits on a flaky-painted chair, coiled around her child. Her arms and her hair, her breasts and her skin, soft as tissue. Smells – like the wind; warmth – like the sun once the winds have died down; slow easy breaths and utter peace – the peace that you feel when it is just you and your child, when it is dark or it is light, when she is soft, velvety-brown and her hair is tightly curled and you, a clouded silhouette, are all she has.

Time that once hung around her like a lead weight assumes a new quality – now time is precious, fought for. Now it is like quicksilver, heavy but elusive and Athene has to chase it, she is afraid that if she does not, she will wake up and it will all have rolled away. Athene looks back on her own childhood and the days were long and slow, they were beautiful and easy and there was no hurry. Time did not have a beginning or an end and there was only the rhythm of the tides or the rhythm of his beating heart when she sat there, on his lap on the veranda, head pressed hard against his chest.

With Iris, Athene finds time brought towards her. Iris puffy limbs blinky eyes squirming seagull crying needs Athene, loves her unconditionally, shows no signs of leaving. There is love here and it is different from her love with the young man but in each she sees the other, in each she sees something of herself and above all, in her love as a mother, she sees a life plotted out for her. She is needed now, noticed now.

How did it feel for Athene – to come back to the bay after all she had gained and all she had lost in the short interval of her absence? At first it was hard for her to analyse – there was too much pressing need in her condition, she was too exhausted. Years of instinct guided her over the stones and round the dunes, over the rocks and through the trees and back to her flaky red cabin – but there were too many other sensations and at first Athene could not stand back, she could not feel how it was to be home.

Later she saw that nothing had changed and that everything had. She came back to the bay and through her mist of fatigue she saw all the same shapes, silhouettes, smelt the same smells. She saw the edge of a piece of cuttlefish jutting through the sand and she thought of the sea-chimes and she knew that it was all there, waiting to be reclaimed.

And yet she saw too that now she could stand outside it all. She could see the bay – for the first time – as others might see it. She could see how small it was, how miniature in the whole scale of the whole island. She could see how wild it was and yet how picturesque – colour of the huts contrasting with endless expanse of the sea; majestic shape of the Lion contrasting with the flat plain of water that surrounded it. She was back where she had been born and she was delighted, elated yes to be here. But now she was no longer inside it and it seemed with this, with the birth of her girl, with all that had happened to her, that she had been granted a reprieve, that the sharp edges of her pains had all been blurred.

Then, a few weeks after the birth, Athene's perceptions are shifted once again. Picture the night that she has when Iris is almost a month old. Hot sea-wind turns to ice sea-wind. Athene sits on her chair and she is dozing off, falling asleep with the slow trance-inducing pull on her breast of a tiny baby. Athene rouses. Her neck is creaking. She drags herself up. Half doped, she makes her way to her bed – too small still – and they curl up lying down now, baby still hanging on, mother drugged with sleep.

In the middle of the night, Athene Brown sits up again – bolt upright. Suddenly she feels the ice sea-wind, she notices the change although it must have happened earlier. She is hot with sweat and cold with sweat. She looks around to find Iris, where is she, is she squashed. Athene's chest is clamp-tight with panic but it is all right she is there and yet she is not there and, worse, there is something else . . .

Athene herself is whirling twirling into life. She is running through it all, those very first moments – as she has just lived them as a mother, only now Athene herself is a baby again, emerging from the darkness of Comfort, being born all over again. Athene feels the rush and the push. She feels the relentless force and the unstoppability and the terror. Years later Athene could look back on the nightmare, stand back from its power, but now Athene is awake and her eyes are wide open and she is reliving it all, wait, stop . . .

. . . and through her own newborn nightmare panic, Athene hears again Comfort's cries, Comfort's gasps, Comfort's need and then her departure, Comfort's gasps, Comfort's slowing breaths, Comfort's silence.

What was it that Athene Brown expected to see when she returned to Samuel's Bay? Throughout the journey that she took, her meandering moon around the island, Athene gave it little thought. There was an instinct guiding her and she trusted it. There was a need to escape the town and a need to put as much distance as she could between her and the body of her lover; between her and the sharp stone and the little girl dirty-dark eyes whose departing back she saw only fleetingly. There was a need to put her head up, above the parapet of her life, and suck in fresh air, new faces.

Athene travelled her land and sometimes she saw it. There were days when she opened her eyes, when she looked up from her work in a field or her work in a barn and she saw the milky beauty of dusk over water; when she was passed by a flock of parrots, hot blue, flying in quick sharp formation. There were days when her belly was reaching out into a huge smile and she felt – down to the very core of her – a growing pull of the land. And then there were days when she could not think, there was no time, and she was driven only by the necessary process of putting one foot in front of another, of travelling from one moment to the next.

Even when she arrived back – when the Lion seemed almost to turn and smile, when the sea roared hello, when the sand blew up in her face and there it was, the little red cabin, there it was, her upturned boat – Athene was unsure why exactly she had come. What sense was there in coming back, in assuming that things would be better since time had elapsed? All that faced her here was a series of circumstances that would be hard for her to overcome – practical knotty detail that she was in no fit state to tackle.

Athene Brown sits in her flaky-painted chair, rocking back and forth, Iris clamped to her chest. Before she had the nightmare, perhaps she would have explained her return in the words of a mother. She would have said I need to go home because I need my child to know me. I need to go back to Samuel's Bay because this is who I am, where I was made, all that I can lay claim to. She would have reasoned too that she had followed her instincts – that she wanted to give roots to her child because somehow she saw herself as uprooted. She wanted to embed her child – Iris's feelings, her dreams, her early happiness – in a place, one place so that Iris could always come back, know the dots on the floor and patterns on the sand and feel this is where I belong. In the words of a mother, Athene would say I have come back because this is where I can be connected, where the line of my forebears can be traced.

And as a person also, as a human being streaked with steely will, perhaps Athene Brown would say I have come back because there is something here I did not finish. Because I wish to walk not an arc but a circle. Athene Brown could say this because she saw the courage of her young man as he died. She saw that he died doing, fighting, that he had not backed away. Even as his followers had capitulated, given in to the demands of their employers, the young man was turning over in his mind how he could try again to win the battle; even as she walked with him to the river and she was waiting to tell him about their

192

child, she could see it now, he was mulling it over, he was looking for ways and means to resolve an issue he believed in profoundly; even again as Athene watched him die – her heart crying out because oh God how much she loved him – she saw that he was thwarted yes but not hiding.

But now that she has had the nightmare, Athene Brown sees there is something else that has brought her back. Something she did not know how much she missed until she saw old Ivy Peacock. Something she did not grant much thought to until she woke up that night, hot with sweat, cold with sweat – and that is Isaiah. What happened to Isaiah? Why did he run away and where did he go to? And how will I find him and is he still alive? And now as Athene asks herself these questions and a host of others along the same lines, she knows she has come back to Samuel's Bay because this too is where she belongs; and because perhaps here, with the eyes of a woman, she might see things, clues, hints that she missed when she was only a child, only struggling to survive on her own.

Does she love him still? Athene Brown struggles to answer that question. It is something she skirts around because it poses too many other problems in its turn. If she loves him still, does he still love her? Would her knack for losing the people she loves rear its head again and she would find him only to lose him once more? And if he does still love her and she still loves him, then why have they not found one another? And why did he leave her, after those bright-garden days, after the storm that she survived and she knows he survived also?

And now that she ponders the loss of Isaiah, she asks herself how her story would have developed if he had stayed. What would she have been if he had not left? What would she have been without Dublin Small and the two Johnnies, without the storm and its sudden shocking consequences, without her battle for the fish and her battle to survive? She had had no hand to reach out to when she almost fell over. She had had no one who knew her from the moment she arrived, knew her hairline and her eyes and what she would say and what she would do. She had had no one to argue with and fight with, no one to be quiet with – and now she sees she has formed a husk of self-sufficiency and it is good to be strong, she believes that, but it is good also to be soft enough to love.

Athene feeds her child, she rights the cabin, she sorts the boat, she makes a crib, she blows away the additional layers of sand that have accrued everywhere since she left, and as she goes she considers how she might find any clues he may have left on his departure. Did he write a note? Did he tell anyone? Did he whisper on the wind that whips the Lion I am going here, I am going this way? She carries Iris strapped to her back or her chest in a tiny warm papoose that she has made from warehouse silk and Athene wonders where to start, how to begin.

She gathers fruit and chops logs and sails out now and again to look for fish and meanwhile her days are peppered with laughter – laughter while her baby smiles, laughter while she makes to sit up for the first time, laughter when Iris finds herself face to face on the sand with a pelican and neither is sure what should happen next. There is rhythm – in her steps, as she marches up and down, Iris warm on her chest, warm on her back, veil over her face to protect her from the wind or the sun, or a hat. Their daytimes are filled with purpose – the sun beating down, the wind rising and falling while together they make the place habitable, restore possessions to the cabin ledges, pick flowers, plant flowers, till and hoe and hammer. And in the evenings, there is rest. Athene sits and carves her sticklebacks – they are becoming more refined now, fragile and yet strong enough to wear round your neck or carry in your pocket. Athene is more ambitious, uses not just tortoiseshell but driftwood or neat slivers of rock. She has increased the range of her tools and the way she uses them and she works quietly, letting the exhaustion ooze from her bones while she plans all of this out, while she looks to a life that can sustain her, her daughter, while she looks to find a way to lure him back.

From time to time, throughout this welter of activity, Athene reflects on how it will be when she finds him again. What will she have to say to someone who ran from her, who left her when he was all she had? What will she say if she finds that someone when throughout her life his abandonment of her has coloured all she has done? Athene might have little Iris asleep in the crook of her knee. She might have her up and over her shoulder while she nurses wind from her belly and she feels the soft ripe smells as they creep down into her lungs. And she will ask herself again, how could he have run – when this is the love that he left behind?

*　　*　　*

The days whip by and slowly things in Samuel's Bay are put to rights. Athene finds a rhythm where she arranges time and sleep, food and pleasure into strict reassuring packets and she watches as her daughter emerges, as a face comes and a person, as movement comes and then words. There are times when she is able to sit, when the sea-chimes blow and her daughter is asleep, when she lights a cheroot or she sucks deep on a glass of home-made Scotch and she might look out from the veranda laden once again with its bumpy rainbow of coloured stones, suck in the expanse of all that sea.

Now her feet sink thuck-thuck into the sand and Iris is bigger, able to walk a little, carry for a while her own weight, so Athene can cast the net of her energy wider, she can resume her mission with the fish. Athene works as she worked once before, only now time is quicker and she works with her child strapped cautiously to her back. She goes out to sea once more in the boat. She seeks out the mothers, tends the mothers, feeds the mothers, tries to kill the predators. She finds that in her absence, things have begun to improve. Whatever it was that was drawing them away – besides the rapacious greed of her predecessors – seems to have subsided and now there are a few shoals here, a few colonies there. She finds too that while once her plan to save the fish was a struggle, desperate fight against the elements and her own childish lack of strength – now, she is buoyed up by the presence of her daughter, by the prospect of seeing Isaiah again, by the fact that somehow the gods are kinder to her, they do not batter her now as they did.

Slowly she finds she can net a few. Once she loads some up in a basket, walks with Iris to the town, offers them in the market – and a man asks if she will sell the stickleback she wears round her neck so Athene sells that too, it was one she had made from a leaf of sandstone she found at the back of the bay and now her life is falling into place, there is trade, there are ideas coming and there are prospects. She will sell fish to the town. If she cannot sell real ones, she will sell her sticklebacks and she will bring home instead books perhaps for her daughter, a bicycle perhaps she has seen one in the town and they will ride together mother and daughter back to the bay, forth from the town. Silk maybe, silk raw so she can show Iris what they made, her young man, the workers, silk and she can let her daughter run her finger over the sheen, bump up and down on the slubs.

And as she rakes back and forth in the waters, back and forth from the town which now is not so far from the bay, Athene comes to realise that she will look for Isaiah where he is most likely to be – perhaps where he has always been, in the bay. She will trawl over every single grain of sand, every single rock, every flower seeking out clues of him, traces of his passing, hints of his presence. Perhaps she believes she will find something tangible – a piece of his clothing, a lock of his hair. Perhaps she will find that note that maybe he did write, maybe he did not. Perhaps she will find something like the pressed flowers of Dublin Small, something that sums up his life and his story, sums up his hopes and his plans, tells her once and for all where he is and when he will return.

Athene begins at the tip of the head of the Lion Rock. She works over every tuft of grass, every tussock, every winnowing billowing blade. She works her way down the rock, face of the Lion with his deep-gouged eyes, and she hunts perhaps just a cell of him, perhaps just a flake of his sun-weathered skin. Slowly she descends, working down into the pools at the Lion's feet, working in and out of his claws, working through the green-lipped mussels which are returning now, in clumps. She finds tiny pieces of glass. She finds feathers. She finds splinters of wood and sometimes she hopes these might belong to him, perhaps broken off from an oar or snagged from his boat but how can she tell after all this time.

Athene moves to the barley-sugar cave. She runs her fingers over the stripes in the ceiling, over the black and the red and the deep gold. She runs her hands over the floor of the cave and it takes her back to the day when they came and told her Dublin had died and she moves deeper, into the dark where prehistoric drips have turned to stone. She turns her attention to the cutty-grass – carefully, it is sharp – and she wonders if these are the same plants that grew under his feet, when he ran here.

The bay too, the waters. The deep pools and the shallow pools, the high tides and the low, the rocks that are sharp and the ones that warm your naked feet and the ones that have been worn smooth by years of pounding from the treacherous seas. They circle the Deadmen – respectfully. They go out to the island where the minke whales still rear their young. They follow the pattern of the colours where the sea turns from amethyst to amber, from azure to black and you see them, Athene Brown upon her boat, Iris strapped to her back, waiting for the wind to abate so they can comb every wave, every catspaw.

All the while Athene shows Iris all that she is tracing for herself. She shows her, for all that the girl is so young, and she watches as the patterns and the shapes and the smells imprint themselves, as the stains and the bumps and the sounds – of a door scraping, of the wind as it whines in a particular corner, of a patch of water as it sucks in and out of the rocks – become part of her daughter's earliest landscape. Athene takes Iris to the bulbous trees at the far end, to the crevasses in the rocks where the agapanthus droop, pendulous under their onion blooms. She takes her up the ridge and down the ridge, in and out of the dunes until everything has been scoured, every grain of sand.

Years later Athene could ask herself whether or not – during those weeks and months when she searched for him – she came any closer to finding out what happened to Isaiah, why he went, where he went, when or whether he might come back. She could ask herself but the answer was not a simple yes or no.

Athene trawled the bay and she found no hint of Isaiah or where he had gone or whether he might return – but she found hints instead of her own story. She found a shell she had engraved with her name one day, when he was out fishing. She found a corner of some cloth of a dress Ivy Peacock had made her and a piece of an old mirror her mother had encrusted with shells and a shard from Dublin's pipe and two matching pairs of gloves, she had made them for the twins, she remembered that now.

She found old smells; she found old sounds; she found old sensations and she gave them to her daughter and too she gave them back to herself.

And in conducting her search, Athene almost rebuilt the bay. She almost constructed it – becoming an artist of the land as she was with her sticklebacks. She relayered all that sand, she restocked all that sea, she built Samuel's Bay and in doing so she came to understand so much more than Isaiah himself, so much more than her own story or that of her daughter. She found piece by piece the intricacy and complexity of Nature and she found that it was in its detail both vast and minute – vast because it preceded her by millennia, vast because at any moment its power could whip up, alter the landscape without warning; minute because what are individuals and their quests for love in comparison with a single bush which has grown here in this sod of earth undaunted since the beginning of time.

Three

Isaiah's health is deteriorating daily. There are moments when he coughs, when he disappears down inside and he wonders if he will ever resurface. At these times Isaiah catches a glimpse of the repose he will be granted when it is all over and you could say the gods are kind, they prepare him for death by making him tired of life.

As death approaches, Isaiah feels more and more like the elephant. Regardless of what he may find when he gets there, he is urgently instinctively driven to return to Samuel's Bay. To return to the grave of his forebears, to return his bones to the place where all the bones of all the fishermen have lain since those of Samuel, ashes blown from the top of the Lion into the sea around. One day Isaiah begins to cough up matter – entwined, he can see, with tiny balls of silk fibre – and Isaiah is not afraid, only knows he must press on.

Before he dies, Isaiah has one remaining desire. He wishes to complete the work in his book. If he is not to know her again, then perhaps she will know him. Perhaps she will find this and perhaps then something will be laid to rest.

*   *   *

Day by day, Isaiah's scrapbook takes on form. The writing becomes more spidery, the words more sparse. The drawings become more abstract – swish-swish-smudge most of the time for Isaiah is weak, enfeebled. But the sense, the journey of his work is returning in on itself. There is a neat loop, the loop of his life and the loop of his journey to and from Samuel's Bay and this Isaiah has managed to capture painstakingly, hauntingly.

As an added challenge to himself, Isaiah has tried to recall all the types of fish that he knew before in Samuel's Bay. He has tried to sum up with one word the essence of the fish, its character; with one or two or at a pinch three strokes of his brush, the look of it. From the smallest to the biggest, from the most humble to the grandest. From the minnow to the tarpon and all the myriad types in between. From the hoki to the tuna, from the sea-roaming whale to the river-hugging salmon. Isaiah finds this search through his deepest memory brings him great comfort. He can dwell for hours on the nature of a particular species. He can go over it, minutely, in his mind – the gills and the whiskers, the scales and the fins. There is a voyage of the imagination and now there is a voyage of recollection.

Sometimes, though it may strike him and others as ironic, Isaiah uses that day of the storm as a reference – there they were laid out all around him, fish from the sea and fish from the rivers that flowed to the sea, all of them sucked up by winds, then thrown down in layers in Samuel's Bay. At the time, Isaiah was traumatised by the storm, by grief, driven to a frenzy by his inability to make a living from the bay – but now he finds that there, from that day, they all lie recorded.

His memory, once consulted, seems fathomless and Isaiah trawls it slowly, lovingly, adding to his work another layer. There is the book of his journey and interleaved there is a kind of encyclopaedia of fish and if you study it, if you look closely at the pages and pore carefully over the drawings, over each one-word stroke that defines a fish or defines a moment in Isaiah's life, you will see this work is crafted mostly from love – its pages imbued with all the craft and care that a simple fisherman can summon in the closing moments of his life.

Follow the contours of the island and you will find Samuel's Bay at the southeastern point. For a long time now, Isaiah has been sailing down the west coast. With the creation of his work and the deepening of his illness, Isaiah has taken his time. The island is not huge yet Isaiah has allowed his journey to last as long as his imagination and his memory might bear fruit. Today Samuel's Bay is all but in sight. The little boat that Isaiah built in the boatyard in the town has crept round that last southernmost promontory and now it is making its way towards the island where the green-lipped mussels used to gather in colonies. In the far distance, if you stand still, look carefully, you can almost catch a first impressive glance of the Lion.

For some reason, after all this time, after all this soul-searching, soul-pacifying time, Isaiah still hesitates before the last run. Perhaps he knows for sure that when he reaches the bay, all will be over. Perhaps he understands that when his work is complete, he will have drawn every last thing inside him out, laid it out on his paper, left himself only empty. Isaiah drops his anchor – the Lion barely discernible in the distance. He finds there is still plenty to do. There is the deck to tidy and the sails to wash and the oars to sand down and a small hole in the hull, he just noticed it last night. There is also his work, one last aspect he wishes to perfect, one last feature in his life Isaiah has yet to summarise with a single word, with a stroke or two of his brush.

The sun is hot and Isaiah works but the beating heat makes him cough badly and Isaiah finds he has no choice, he has to move on a little further, seek some shade. Isaiah pulls up his anchor. He lets the little boat go and it takes him – while he coughs almost uncontrollably, almost definitively – sure enough to the dark deep pool that sits just beyond the Deadmen. There, there is a light breeze. There the Lion casts just enough shade for him to breathe once more and after all Isaiah is pleased, it means he can see the great rock from up close, etch in more particularly the lines around its gouged-out eyes.

So now it is a hot day in a miraculously hot spring. Here, where the seasons are normally temperate, where the climate is lush and the flora is lush and the sea is stirred by semi-tropical winds, Isaiah pulls out his book, his table, his chair. He sets down the chair in the fragment of hot-spring shade and he begins to work on the one last person he has not yet dared to encounter in his memory. Dot-spot-swish and you see a child. Dot-spot-swish and for sure it must be a girl. In the distance, a school of flying fish leaps from the water, silver threading hoop-la splintering into a thousand flashes in the sunlight, but Isaiah cannot look, he is too involved in his work.

At last the sun is overhead and there is no more shade. Coughing disturbs Isaiah as he works. It racks his thin, elderly sea-worn frame until you can almost hear the sound from the other side of the bay. Coughing finally brings his work to a halt, forces him to leave his book open, page incomplete while Isaiah goes to rest, while Isaiah sits back, on his chair. In the droplets of peace hard-won in this growing battle between life and death, Isaiah finds himself going back to the Carnival of the Fish, to that day when he was a boy and his father held his hand. Isaiah's eyes are closed. In the distance, he believes he can hear those strings of cuttlefish, leaves of mica, ringing then and always with the sound of the sea.

Four

C risp and brilliant, the dawn. Athene Brown wakes her daughter. Today it is hot – one in a succession of hot spring days they have just enjoyed – and there is no wind, none at all. Today, Athene says to herself, they are going to play the game she used to play with Dublin Small. They will climb the cutty-grass hill. She will teach Iris the trick that Dublin taught her all those years before and they will sit there, mother and daughter silhouetted on the slope, listening to the picture of the bay and the rhythms of the planet, listening to the sea and the wind and the fish, threading in and out of the waves.

Now it is several years since the young man died. Athene remembers him when she looks in Iris's eyes sometimes, when Iris does something and it has just the ring of him. Her memory of him was always untarnished and now it has assumed a kind blur. There was love and it was good and now there is Iris and she is good also.

In Iris, Athene thinks too that she catches hints of her own father – hints of Isaiah's build, that mannerism he had of pointing one foot when he stood still; hints of his laugh which she hears as it rings back down through the years and she is there again, holding his hand, shadowing his every move.

Nothing in Athene's search has given her to believe Isaiah will return. She has found nothing – not a trace of him, not a hint – for all that her search has been relentless, indeed, may never be completed. And yet everything she has done in her search has helped Athene to understand why it was that Isaiah left. If she did not know before when she lived here alone, she knows now how hard it must have been for him: for a young man to take the place of a mother, act the father, grieve for the grandfather, work on the sea. How hard it must have been to show love, real undying love on the one hand – and yet to let it go on the other.

Athene herself struggles with the same battle day to day. She has to let go of her love for the young man, leader of the silk workers; yet all the while she must cling on to the joy she derives from seeing or holding or even smelling her child. There are times during this battle when Athene feels she may not after all be equal to it – perhaps Iris is crying inconsolably and she looks just as he did and the wind is blowing, sand stinging their faces; perhaps she dreams of him, of his light touch, and it is almost as though he is there, with her, and how can she bear for it not to be true.

Nor have the gods forgotten their old trick of being troublesome to Athene, bringing her problems just when she thought she had everything under control. Perhaps she draws in empty nets and she wonders if there are fishermen out there, thwarting her attempts at custodianship; perhaps a shark gets in, a predator, breaks through the nets she has drawn across parts of the sound and she is obliged to force him out or worse still to kill him because how else will they restore the bay to its old splendour; perhaps she is forced to doubt the wisdom of her mission as once happened when some leery townsfolk came and threatened to join her, to set up home here because they had heard there might be rich pickings and Athene had to scream out no, she had to whisper soft no, regain her reason, explain that there are no fish now, only seaweed, no prospects, only sea-winds.

But somehow for Athene, the battle is not so hard-fought. She herself does not understand why but for the most part she tries to revel in the good. She makes her sticklebacks, taking exquisite, minute pleasure in each one – each one different and yet each bearing unimpeachable witness to that first fish that landed on her lap all those years before. Every month, they cycle to the town and she sells them in the market and they bring home things that they need and, sometimes, things that they want.

With the sale of the sticklebacks, Athene finds she need not worry so much about the fish in the sea. There are times for sure when she chases off sharks, when she tries to tend the beds or she rows out, bait-bag in hand, trying to lure more back; and it takes her several years before she lets down the nets – but she finds her own efforts did not make too much difference. At times, they seemed to return, no faster or slower than she could make them, and at others, they seemed to disappear again. For this, Athene feels in turn appalled that the bay will never recover its old glory and relieved at least that the bay is home now only to her and to Iris.

But above all, Athene finds she can take pleasure in her daughter – in the little feet that step into her footprints; in the small voice that echoes hers; in the moments they share together, when they sit on the veranda, the one enfolded in the other, and look out, over the lilac counterpane that rolls lace-fringed before them.

Today, hot-spring day, little wind, is a perfect day to play the listening game. Athene holds Iris's hand and together they mount the slope. The sun is climbing. The shadows are decreasing in size and soon Iris is running ahead, shouts beat you when she reaches the clearing.

Soon Athene catches up and they crouch down. The grass is dry and sharp and they have to be careful where they crouch because it crick-cracks beneath them and then they will have to start all over again, trying to be dead dead silent all over again. You have to go almost into a trance, says Athene. You have to empty your head and your ideas and forget everything, the time, where we are, what you see, Iris. All that you do, Iris, is listen. Wait and see what you hear.

Iris tries and hears the beating of her heart. She tries again and she thinks she hears a beastie, is it a fly, buzzing round her head. Then she tries again, really, really still and she says I can hear it Ma, I can hear the grass on top of the Lion, I can hear it blow.

Athene does not answer. Iris opens her eyes and she sees her mother is still there, only she does not answer. Athene

210

is deep, rapt in her trance. Iris is frightened, she shakes her mother. She shakes her again and Athene feels it, she feels her little diamond girl pulling on her.

But what is there to say when she has heard him. Over the bright white sea, over the iron-black sand, down the long shimmering ribbon of memory, in and out of the tears of childhood, up to now here, among the winnowing grass, hot-spring day, sea-chimes ringing in the distance, she has heard him.

Iris runs down the hill behind her mother but she does not cry out wait for me, she only follows on. She watches as Athene runs down the grass, bare feet being cut, she does not care. She watches her feet hit the sand with a big jump at the bottom, watches her as her hair streams out behind her while her legs propel her through the water, round the Lion Rock, out towards the Deadmen. She watches her out of sight . . .

. . . and years later – as she takes her turn in the flaky-painted chair on the veranda in the blood-red hut with the velvet-brown fedora hanging on the hook and Isaiah's sketchbook sitting on the shelf, as she turns her cowrie-shell bracelet on her wrist while the wind-up gramophone warbles on the table and the cuttlefish-chimes hang in the door, ringing then and always with the sound of the sea – Iris recalls that picture she has of her mother with Isaiah: Athene first as she swims, then as she wades; Athene with her sequin-covered scarf trailing in the waves, dark with water; Athene reaching the old man, leap-frogging over the side of the boat, he is there in his chair, eyes closed, ribs jutting in ladders . . .

And then together, when the sea-dark sky has swallowed the waters, as she leads him slowly inland, as she part lifts, part drags him up to the top of the Lion and they make a bonfire, adding fish-oil and seaweed to the flames – and then they sit and they watch as million-coloured sparks blow and flicker out over the night sea.

CHARLOTTE FAIRBAIRN

God Breathes His Dreams Through Nathaniel Cadwallader

A spellbinding story of belief, superstition and innocence lost.

In an outlying village in a far-away valley, rumours have begun to spread: a mysterious figure has been sighted, astride a magnificent stallion. Could this be the man the villagers have been praying for, come to lead them through their hour of need?

Nathaniel Cadwallader's arrival does indeed usher in a golden age of faith and tranquility. Yet there are those who resent this gentle, aloof craftsman and the ease with which he holds the community in the palm of his hand. When a beautiful outsider attempts to claim Nathaniel as her own, the spell is broken, and he quickly becomes a scapegoat for his detractors' own guilt and fears.

'A poetic allegory with hints of Thomas Hardy and a dash of magic realism, the book is about the divine nature of art, and is set in an entirely imaginary countryside, described in vivid beauty and harshness' *Harpers and Queen*

'An imaginative tale of a world which time forgot, loss of innocence and the devastation of betrayal' *Buzz* Magazine

'Richly imagined' *Scotsman*

'A completely gripping story that holds the reader entranced until the end . . . Reading this book is a powerful experience not to be missed' *Amazon.co.uk*

0 7553 0183 8

review

You can buy any of these other **Review** titles from your bookshop or *direct from the publisher*.

FREE P&P AND UK DELIVERY
(Overseas and Ireland £3.50 per book)

A History of Forgetting	Caroline Adderson	£6.99
The Catastrophist	Ronan Bennett	£6.99
The Mariner's Star	Candida Clark	£6.99
Hallam Foe	Peter Jinks	£6.99
This is Not a Novel	Jennifer Johnston	£6.99
The Song of Names	Norman Lebrecht	£6.99
In Cuba I was a German Shepherd	Ana Menéndez	£6.99
The Secret Life of Bees	Sue Monk Kidd	£6.99
My Lover's Lover	Maggie O'Farrell	£6.99
Early One Morning	Robert Ryan	£6.99
Missing	Mary Stanley	£6.99
The Hound in the Left-Hand Corner	Giles Waterfield	£6.99
God Breathes His Dreams Through Nathaniel Cadwallader	Charlotte Fairbairn	£6.99

TO ORDER SIMPLY CALL THIS NUMBER

01235 400 414

or visit our website: www.madaboutbooks.com

Prices and availability subject to change without notice.